BURNING SECRETS

NASHVILLE IMMORTALS BOOK 3

SHAUNA JARED

burning secrets

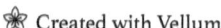

DEDICATION

For Jeff and Gunnar. I love you both so much. Thank you for supporting me and my dreams!

To my alpha and beta readers, thank you for reading and for your feedback and support. I appreciate you all so much!

1

      "Another round for my girls!" I yelled to the bartender over the sounds of the country music band playing in the corner of the little Honky Tonk bar as I adjusted my cowboy hat. He nodded in confirmation, and I let my body sway to the music while I waited. I looked over my shoulder, flipping my long blonde hair aside as I did. The girls, Essie and Doreen, waved to me from our little table in the back. I grinned at them and turned back to the bartender.

    The song ended as the bartender passed the drinks to me. "Here you go, Cricket," he said with a wink. I laid a few bills on the counter for him, which included a generous tip since Tom always gave me one "on the house." I carefully gathered the drinks amid applause and whoops from the audience for the band, then headed toward the girls.

    I drunkenly navigated the path from the bar to our table, being careful with the drinks, as the music started up again. It was Girl's Night Out for the three of us, and it was long overdue. So much had happened in my life recently. I needed a relaxing night out with friends and a few drinks.

First of all, I had gotten fired from my job as a paralegal, which led to my employment as a Daytime Concierge for vampires. My vampire boss at the time was cursed with mortality and forced me to help her find a way to reverse it by kidnapping my teenage daughter. In the meantime, a hot Grim Reaper named Zeb had moved in next door to me, and together, we saved my daughter. The vampire? Not so lucky.

Only a few months later, I was kidnapped by a raging Alpha werewolf who demanded I help him revive a defunct supernatural drug cartel using my newfound Revealer abilities. The Alpha? The brother of my best friend Joey, who was also a werewolf. Joey and Zeb found me, but not before the Alpha slapped me around a bit. And that was only the tip of the iceberg of what I'd been through recently.

I definitely needed a drink. Or a few.

As I approached our table, I noticed a man with a dark blond crew cut sitting in my spot next to Essie. He wore a suit and a seductive smile as his eyes focused on Essie's. She shot him a smirk, her smokey eyes darkening and her red lips curling as her gaze raked him up and down. Doreen sat there, vaping and looking the other way, giving a little smile and a wave to someone across the room.

My smile faltered as I grew closer and realization dawned on me. I picked up the faint scent of smoke with a metallic undertone to it, making me stop in my tracks. I recognized it.

Aiden Rhys. The dragon shifter.

"Shug, let me help you with those drinks!" Doreen yelped, jumping up and grabbing the Long Island Iced Tea and the Jack and Coke out of my precarious grasp, leaving me with only my Bud Light as I stared at Aiden.

Essie glanced past Aiden at me, her brows knit together

as she took her drink from Doreen. "Are you okay, mate?" she asked in her smooth Australian accent, as I stared at Aiden. She glanced at him and then back at me with a raised eyebrow.

I gathered myself quickly. "Yeah, I'm great!" I replied a little too enthusiastically, raising my beer to her in a toast. Aiden looked at me then, the corner of his mouth turning up in a sly smile.

"Cricket Jones, if memory serves me?" he asked, standing and motioning for me to take the seat which had been mine in the first place. He moved back so I could sit down next to Essie, who still looked between us with a frown. He swiped a chair from the neighboring table and brought it to ours, where he sat down again. Doreen took a drag from her vaping device and grinned.

"You remember, Aiden, right Cricket? We met him at The Rusty Nail awhile back," Doreen said in her raspy voice and blew some vapors in the other direction. *As if I could forget a dragon shifter.*

"Of course, I remember. Hey, Aiden. Funny meeting you here tonight." I narrowed my eyes at him as I took a pull from my beer. Aiden Rhys had approached Doreen and me not long ago at the bar where Joey worked. He asked to buy us a drink, and when I shook his hand, my Revealer senses took over, telling me what he was. I had excused myself as quickly as I could, not knowing what to make of a dragon shifter appearing here in Nashville.

I'd found some unsettling information on dragon shifters in one of the books my mentor, Gus, gave me since meeting with Aiden. I knew dragons lived together in Draconian "clutches" with other dragon shifters, that they collected and hoarded gold and other treasures, and they were notoriously devious.

Since I hadn't seen or heard of any other dragon shifters in the Metropolitan Nashville area lately, I assumed Aiden was here alone, and that was worrisome. Why was he here, and what did he want? One thing was certain—I didn't trust him. So, I had done what I thought was the right thing to do at the time. I alerted my vampire boss, Carl, the Director of the Nashville chapter of the Ministry of Vampire Affairs. Since he'd hired me to use my Revealer powers to determine why numerous supernatural creatures had been migrating to the Nashville area over the last several years, I figured it was my duty to let him know.

Carl was livid.

Which had left me with a new assignment: Find out what Aiden Rhys's business was in Nashville. And I'd been trying to since meeting Aiden, but there had been no trace of him anywhere. Until tonight.

Aiden studied me, a small smile playing on his lips. "Yes, what a coincidence. 'Of all the gin joints in all the towns in all the world...'" he said in a deep-voiced southern accent, raising the glass of whiskey to his mouth and winking at me so subtly I almost missed it.

But was it a coincidence that he was here? I wasn't sure if Aiden knew about my supernatural radar detector abilities or not. Was running into him here tonight at the bar an accident? Or an orchestrated plan on his part? I had no way of knowing. I watched with trepidation as he turned his attention back to Essie. I was going to have to warn her about him before he charmed the pants right off her, I thought while watching her laugh flirtatiously.

I was glaring at Aiden and ignoring Doreen's chatter when my phone vibrated. I pulled it out of my back pocket to see who it was. Joey. I smiled as I swiped to open the message, my previous worries about Aiden evaporating for the moment.

Hey babe, what RU up 2 tonite?

> Girls Night Out. When are you coming
> back btw?

After Joey's brother, Drake, had been abjured by their pack and forced to resign as Alpha, Joey had taken the reins as an "Interim Alpha" until the pack could get back on its feet. That meant he'd had to go back to his hometown of New Haven, Kentucky, and I missed him like crazy. I couldn't even go to The Rusty Nail now without thinking about him, which was why we weren't there tonight.

Wait... U don't miss me, do U? ;)

> Maybe. But only a little.

LOL behave 2nite babe

> Never. I'll call you soon!

I put my phone away, a little smile on my lips when I looked up to see Doreen grinning like a Cheshire cat and bouncing her leg to the music.

"What?" I asked, irritated. I knew exactly what she was thinking, and I wasn't in the mood.

"Was that Joey? Or Zeb? I'm telling ya, Cricket, I don't know how you do it. Two of the hottest men I've ever seen in my life, and you've got 'em both eating out of your hand. You go, girl," she said in her throaty southern accent, taking a pull from her vaping device. Tonight's flavor was called "The Pursuit of Happiness."

I rolled my eyes at her. Doreen was in her 50s and always dressed to impress. Tonight, she was clad in a denim skirt and matching denim jacket, with hot pink tights and a metallic bow in her hair, circa 1986. Her blonde hair was teased stiff with hairspray, her eyelids covered in baby blue eyeshadow, and a pastel pink shade adorned her lips. If the 1980s ever had a poster child, Doreen was it.

I sighed. "It was Joey. And we're just friends." I retrieved my now lukewarm beer and took a swig.

She nodded, giving me a knowing look. "Okay, if you say so, hun. Oh, there's Cindy! I'll be right back!" she exclaimed, then rushed off in Cindy's direction, whoever she was.

I glanced at Aiden and Essie, who were sitting way too close together, engaged in a conversation I couldn't hear. I cleared my throat, which they ignored. Aiden reached out to tuck a lock of Essie's platinum blonde hair behind her ear, and she gave him a sultry smile in return.

Okay, that was enough.

"So, Aiden, where are you from? What do you do for a living?" I asked loudly so they couldn't ignore me this time. Essie gave me a "WTF" look, and I shrugged, turning my attention to Aiden.

Aiden tore his gaze from Essie and turned to me. His golden skin seemed to glow under the bar's lighting, and his chiseled jawline only accentuated the smirk he sent my way. "I'm from Atlanta. I work for my father's company as an Antiques Acquisition Agent, which is just a fancy way of saying I collect old shit," he said, lifting his tumbler of whiskey to his lips.

Essie erupted into laughter at that. "That's so cool, I love it!" she exclaimed, caressing his arm.

I rolled my eyes. "Antiques? Well, Nashville is full of them. I'm sure you'll find plenty here. Doesn't Atlanta have any 'old shit'?" I asked with narrowed eyes while peeling the label from my bottle of Bud.

He laughed before downing what was left of his whiskey and setting the glass on the table, his eyes glinting with mischief. "There's plenty of old shit in Atlanta, too. But I'm searching for something in particular for a client, and I have it on good authority that I might find it here."

"So, what is it? This thing you're looking for?" Essie asked, her eyes widening as she finished her drink. It was apparent to anyone with half a brain that she was utterly taken with him.

He leaned closer and whispered, "Can't tell you, darlin'. It's top secret." Then he sent her a wink, which made her laugh again, a tinkling little high-pitched sound that grated on my nerves.

My displeasure must have been apparent because Aiden cocked his head toward me and said, "I'm sorry, Cricket, have I done something to offend you?"

Essie turned to me with a "how dare you" look on her face, her darkening emerald eyes accusing me of ruining this for her. "You have been acting a little aggy tonight, Cricket. What gives?"

I sighed. Obviously, our Girl's Night Out was over, now that Aiden had shown up. I was aggravated, irritated, and my buzz was long gone. "You know what, I think I'm just gonna head home. Why don't you come with me?" I grabbed my crossbody bag from the back of my chair.

"No! Cricket! What's gotten into you, mate?" Essie asked, watching me with confusion. I glanced at Aiden. His eyes followed me as I gathered my things. A smug smile formed on his lips, and I felt like punching him all of a sudden. Honestly, even I was a little taken aback at how strongly I disliked the guy. Maybe Mercury was in retrograde or something.

"Nothing, I just feel like going home now. I'm gonna go find Doreen. You staying?" I stood and paused for her answer. I figured Aiden would pipe up to offer her a ride home if she wanted to stay, which he did.

Essie glanced at him apologetically, then back to me. "Wait, I'll go with you."

I blinked in surprise as my heart swelled a bit. I had never really known where I stood with Essie all this time, although I considered her a friend. She was a Grim Reaper, just like Zeb, and they were close friends. Several times during the events of the past few months, Essie questioned my loyalty to Zeb and got angry with me. And she had every right. My head had been a mess while Zeb was out of town, and I let my relationship with Joey cross over the friendship line. I had been completely honest with Zeb about it all, though, and I assumed Essie had just let bygones be bygones for his sake, but now… Essie was picking me over Aiden. Even though I was being bitchy for no apparent reason. I'd always heard about it, but without many female friends, I'd never experienced it. The Girl Code.

I wanted to throw my arms around Essie and plant a big kiss on her cheek. Instead, I tossed my long blonde hair over my shoulder and sent a smug look Aiden's way while I waited for Essie to gather her black bag, which was covered in silver buckles and fringe, along with her black leather jacket. Cricket 1, Aiden 0. I smiled.

Aiden pursed his lips, took out his wallet, and pulled out a business card. He held it out to Essie when she looked up. "Give me a call sometime. Maybe you can show me around town and help me find some 'old shit.'" She smiled and took the card while he glared at me as if to say Cricket 1, Aiden 1. I glared right back.

"Bye, Aiden," I called, taking Essie by the arm and practically dragging her along with me to find Doreen while she tried to wave goodbye to him. Essie and I were going to have a serious talk about the dragon shifter.

2

After dropping off Essie and Doreen, I arrived at the duplex to find my living room window lit with a faint yellow glow, and I could tell the television was on from the pulsating, colorful lights that came and went. I smiled, looping my crossbody bag over my head and making my way to the front door.

I unlocked the door as quietly as possible, then I crept inside, depositing my bag and keys on the kitchen counter. I entered the living room to find Zeb stretched out on the recliner portion of the couch in my living room, wearing a flannel shirt with a half-eaten bowl of popcorn sitting on the floor. A few beer bottles littered the coffee table, and he still held the remote control in his hand. I grinned, sitting down beside him and laying my head on his chest.

Although Zeb technically lived on the other side of the duplex that my Grandma Betty owned, he'd been living in my half of it for all intents and purposes recently, only returning to his side when he needed clothes or some of his Reaper gear. I loved having him here every night, although my teenage daughter probably wouldn't agree. Mackenzie, who went by Mac, liked to complain about Zeb being here all the time, but I believed she secretly enjoyed having him around since her dad, my ex-husband, was out of town.

Zeb stirred when I snuggled closer to him, his large muscular arms enveloping me. He groaned and glanced at the clock on the wall. "You're home early, Princess. How was Girl's Night?" He planted a kiss on top of my head.

"Great, at first. Do you remember the dragon shifter I told you about?" I asked, basking in the warmth of his body heat as he held me close.

"I do. What's he got to do with anything?" Zeb asked in his deep British accent. His muscles tensed.

I lifted my head up to look at him. "Aiden. That's his name. He showed up at the bar and had Essie swooning over him. The guy is smooth, I'll give him that." I rolled my eyes and waited for a response.

Zeb relaxed as he chuckled. "Essie? Swooning? Now that I'd like to see."

"I'm not kidding. It was disturbing."

He pulled me close and kissed me softly. "Sounds like you need a distraction," he said, kissing me again. I smiled against his lips, then groaned as I heard footsteps coming down the stairs behind us.

I twisted around to see Mac bounding down the stairs, her long black hair loose and trailing behind her. She wore gray pajama pants covered in black cats wearing witch hats, and a black T-shirt that read "#bookish."

She stopped, spotting us on the couch, her face screwing up in disgust. "Gross," she decided, then continued on to the kitchen.

I turned to Zeb and deadpanned, "Isn't she precious?"

He laughed. "That she is."

Mac came back into the living room with a bottle of

water, then paused at the stairs. "If you can take a short break from examining Zeb's tonsils with your tongue, maybe we could talk about my birthday party?"

My brows knit in confusion as I turned to face her. "Party? You never want a party. I thought you said birthday parties were a social construct designed to promote self-aggrandizement? Or something like that?" I asked, not remembering the exact details of that particular rant. She rolled her eyes and marched over to us, where she threw herself down on the other side of the L-shaped couch.

"Mom, I'm turning sixteen. I think a little self-aggrandizement is in order," she said, scowling at me while twisting the cap off the water and taking a sip.

Zeb sat up, effectively dumping me off his chest. "I agree. Sixteen is a milestone. It should be celebrated. What kind of party did you have in mind, Mac?" he asked her.

I grinned, excited he was taking an interest in Mac. Zeb had never been around kids before, much less teenagers, so he was still a bit awkward with her. It made me happy to see him making an effort.

"Let's hear it," I added, sitting back on the couch and stifling a yawn.

Mac beamed. "I'm thinking—Victorian Gothic. Regina and I found this gorgeous black lace Victorian gown I could wear. And we could decorate with black roses, lace doilies, candles, stuff like that. What do you think?" she asked, biting her lip.

"So, black everything then?" I asked.

She shot me an incredulous look while scoffing. "Mom."

"I think it sounds lovely, Mac. Perfect for your birthday," Zeb said, beaming at her.

I raised an eyebrow at him and smiled softly. "Actually, I agree. Let's do it," I concluded, turning to Mac.

She looked pleased, although I could tell she was trying hard not to. "Awesome. Thanks, Mom! And Zeb," she added after a brief pause, jumping up to give me a rare hug. Startled, I hugged her back. Then, she was up the stairs in a black and gray blur, her bedroom door slamming behind her.

I glanced at Zeb and chuckled.

"What?" he asked, his face going rosy. His spiky blond hair was disarrayed from his impromptu nap, his piercing blue eyes meeting mine while a grin tugged at his lips.

"You know what. You and Mac, that's what," I said. He rolled his eyes, and I continued, "I think it's sweet, that's all. And I appreciate the effort. It means a lot." I leaned in and placed a soft kiss on his pouty lips.

"Oh? And just how much do you appreciate it, Princess?" He waggled his eyebrows. I laughed, and before I could reply, my cell phone chimed with a text message. I frowned and grabbed my phone.

"It's Carl. He's been in a tizzy about Aiden ever since I told him there was a dragon shifter in our midst," I said, typing a quick message back to my boss. I was used to the late-night texts from him since vampires worked the night shift. I needed to go in one night soon and update Carl on Aiden, but I wanted to find out more first. So far, the only information I'd gathered was that he was an antique dealer from Georgia. I needed more.

Zeb's arms snaked around my waist as I texted. He pulled me close, kissing up my neck, sending shivers and heat simultaneously through my body. I bit my lip while I finished the message to Carl, then tossed the phone aside. I turned to him, letting my hands roam up his muscular, tattooed arms, over his broad shoulders, and into his hair as we kissed. A moan escaped my lips as he teased and tortured me.

It was so easy to be with Zeb. He made me feel sexy and fun, and we fit so well together. We'd been together now for several months, aside from the few weeks where he had literally gone to Hell to find a way out of his Grim Reaper duties. During that time, I had no idea where he was or what he was doing. I had been so worried, and I'd thought the worst—that he was either dead or cheating on me. In the meantime, I'd also gotten closer to Joey. A lot closer. Which had left my heart torn in two, each of them claiming a piece.

After Zeb came back and I'd recovered from my time spent in the company of Joey's vindictive brother, Drake, Joey had willingly stepped aside, so I didn't have to make a difficult choice. He had to go back to Kentucky for a while anyway to tend to his pack and the mess left behind after Drake had been dethroned as Alpha. He knew my feelings for Zeb were strong. Joey's wolf side had imprinted on me, and I still wasn't sure exactly what that entailed, but it meant Joey made a tremendous sacrifice by letting me go.

But I hadn't let go. Not yet. Each of them still held a piece of my heart, and I desperately tried to ignore the part that still belonged to Joey. Zeb knew what happened while he was away and how I felt about Joey. He didn't like it, but he understood. So, here I was, attempting to stuff Joey back into the friendship box while taking my relationship with Zeb to the next level. And still unsure if it was the right thing to do.

My thoughts raced and my heart squeezed, thinking about my feelings for both of them, while Zeb and I continued making out on the couch. Finally, it was too much. I couldn't do this tonight, not after letting my thoughts go down that rabbit hole. I pulled back from Zeb with one final kiss, my hands resting on his chest. My Revealer senses picked up the dry, crackling heat surrounding Zeb, a mixture of his Reaper aura and his desire for me.

His brows furrowed as his gaze met mine. "Is anything wrong?" he asked, raising an eyebrow.

I shook my head and smiled. "No, I'm fine. I think the alcohol and excitement from tonight are just catching up with me." I took his hand, giving it a squeeze, and he smiled in relief.

God, I loved him, even though I still hadn't said it out loud. And that made me feel even more guilt about the feelings I still harbored for Joey.

"Understandable. It's late anyway. Let's call it a night then, shall we?" he asked, standing and pulling me to my feet. He wrapped me in a warm embrace and kissed my forehead, taking my hand and leading me toward the staircase. I followed him up to the bedroom, grateful for the rest and relief that sleep would soon grant.

———

THE NEXT DAY, Mac and I sat at the kitchen table, my laptop open with Pinterest pulled up. We each had coffee in hand while searching for ideas for Mac's Victorian Gothic party. It seemed my original hypothesis regarding the theme had been correct—everything black. Black roses, black tablecloths, black lace, black candles, black dresses. She even showed me a black birthday cake with dark purple buttercream roses. I didn't even want to imagine what my teeth would look like after one bite of that thing.

After concluding everything at the party should be

black, we moved on to the guest list. Among them, her best friend, Regina, and Mac's boyfriend, Luther. She decided to invite a few other friends from school, and then we moved on to the longer list of family and my friends.

"Zeb will be there, of course. And Grandma and Gus. I'll ask Doreen and Essie, too," I said as I wrote the names down on a legal pad. "I wonder if Joey could come?" I bit the end of the ink pen before writing his name down with a question mark next to it.

"Don't forget Dad," Mac added, watching me write. I paused. John-Clarke had been in Bitter End recently after an extended absence and rekindled his relationship with his estranged daughter. He also somehow managed to get involved with a supernatural drug cartel while he was in town. His penance for his role in getting me kidnapped was that he had to stay with the endangered pixies, keeping them safe, until they were settled in and we were sure the threat to them was eliminated. But Mac didn't know that. All she knew was that I had helped her dad get a job, and he had to go out of town for work. She'd been upset when he left and blamed me for sending him away.

I didn't think there was any way John-Clarke could come back for the party, but how to tell her that? Besides, even if he was free, he'd probably just return to his flighty ways, and Mac wouldn't see him again for another eighteen months. It was easier to just let her blame me instead of letting her dad break her heart again.

I grimaced. "I doubt your dad will be able to get away from work, Mac. I'm sorry. I know you'd like for him to be here. How about this—we'll plan a small belated birthday party for when he gets back?" I mentally crossed my fingers that she'd go for it.

Mac pursed her lips and returned her gaze to Pinterest.

Her green eyes flared and her brows drew together as she scrolled violently through pin after pin. Oh boy, here it comes. She flipped her black locks over her shoulder and turned to face me, finally.

"So, not only did you manage to get him a job that would take him away from Bitter End, you've also arranged it so that he can't take time off to come to his own daughter's sixteenth birthday party?" she asked, narrowing her eyes at me. I bit my lip. "Why are you so petty, Mom?" She stared me down.

I closed my eyes briefly and took a deep breath. I reminded myself it was better for her if I just allowed her to blame me. She didn't need to know about the supernatural world, and she didn't need John-Clarke to break her heart again. Then I conjured up a mental image of me strangling John-Clarke, which made me feel a little better. I decided to keep that image on my mental pinboard, ready to meditate on whenever I needed it. He wasn't even here, and he was stressing me out.

"I didn't 'arrange' anything, Mac. His job took him out of town, that's it. His assignment won't be over in time for your birthday party. I'm sorry." I really did feel bad that he wouldn't be able to make it, for her sake. He may have made my life a living hell while we were married and left me with a mountain of debt and a teenage daughter to raise on my own when we divorced, but he was Mac's Dad, the only one she'd ever have, and she loved him.

"Why can't you ask your boss to let him come home? Just for one weekend? Please?" she begged. She was killing me.

I grabbed her hand and squeezed. "It doesn't work that way, sweetie. I'm sorry." She quickly withdrew her hand from mine and pushed away from the table. With a scathing look at me, she bolted up the stairs to her bedroom, slamming the door behind her, but not before I spotted her eyes shimmering with unshed tears. *Damn it, John-Clarke.* I slammed my laptop shut and put my head in my hands. My phone rang, playing "Bad Chick" by SoMo.

"Hi, Grandma."

"Cricket! Are you okay?" Grandma asked in her shrill voice.

I held the phone away from my ear for a moment before answering her. "Yes. Why wouldn't I be?" I countered. I rubbed my temples and pressed the phone to my ear with my shoulder while I put my laptop away.

Grandma huffed. "Well, since you never call or come by anymore, I have no way of knowing if you're okay or not, do I?"

I rolled my eyes. "I'm sorry, Grandma. I've been busy. Do you need something, or did you just call to make me feel bad? If that's the case, get in line."

"I do need something. I need you to come over as soon as you can. There's something I need to talk to you about," she said, whispering that last part.

I frowned. "Oh, God. Are you marrying Gus?" I paused in the middle of clearing our coffee mugs from the table and pictured the two eighty-somethings walking down the aisle together in the chapel at Forever Young. Now that I thought about it, though, that wouldn't be so bad. Gus had grown on me.

"No!"

"Why can't you tell me over the phone then?"

"Cricket, just come over. Why do you have to be so difficult?"

I sighed. I'd been called "petty" and "difficult" within the last five minutes, and it wasn't even noon yet.

"Fine. I'll come over as soon as I can. This had better be good, though," I said, a warning tone in my voice. "By the way, we're throwing a birthday party for Mac in two weeks. Wear black."

"Black? That's so last season, Cricket. I'll wear my new hot pink tracksuit."

"That will match the Victorian Gothic theme to a T," I said, exasperated with her. I just wanted to hang up now.

"Victorian Gothic? Is that a rock group?" she asked, bewildered.

"No, Grandma. Wear whatever you want, just come to the party. I have to go."

"No need to get snippy, Cricket. Don't forget to come over!"

"Bye, Grandma." I pressed the "end call" button before she had a chance to object.

3

———————

I spent most of the following week preparing for Mac's birthday party and avoiding Grandma Betty. Since it was such short notice and I had a "connection" at The Rusty Nail—aka, Joey—we decided to have it there on Saturday afternoon before the place started getting busy. I went to every store in Metro Nashville purchasing black cups, paper plates, napkins, candles, streamers, roses, and anything else I could think of that came in black. I'd even ordered the black cake with dark purple flowers for her. Doreen and I went to The Nail early on the day of the party to decorate, and when we finished, I had to admit it didn't look half bad.

"HGTV, eat your heart out. This is 'Victorian Gothic on a Budget,'" I said, grinning from ear to ear and taking in all of our hard work. I glanced at Doreen, who looked pleased as well.

"Shug, I had my doubts we could pull it off, but you made it happen. Mac is gonna love it!" Doreen sat at a booth with black and purple flowers as a centerpiece and black and silver glitter on the tablecloth. She took a pull from her vaping device, loaded with "Gothic Dreams" for the occasion.

"I really hope you're right, Doreen. She's kinda pissed at me right now about John-Clarke not being able to come." I glanced at the time on my phone. "I'd better go put on my Victorian gown and get ready. Guests will be arriving soon." I grabbed my duffel bag full of clothes and makeup and headed to the restroom.

I donned my fancy black lace antique dress that Mac had brought home the night before. According to her, she and Regina had found an old trunk full of treasures at a local thrift store. They'd bought it and taken it to Regina's house to sort through it, and this dress, among many other things, had been inside. I turned around in the small bathroom, checking myself out in the mirror. The dress fit me well, accentuating my curves in all the right places. *Zeb will definitely like this*. I pulled my long blonde hair up into a loose bun, letting a few tendrils spill out to frame my face. Then I applied my makeup according to Mac's instructions, which meant heavily smoked eyes and dark red lipstick.

Finally, I figured I was as ready as I could be, so I emerged from the restroom to find a few guests had already arrived, along with Zeb, Mac, Regina, and Luther. As predicted, Zeb's jaw dropped when he spotted me in the dress, and I did a little twirl for him, giving him a sultry stare.

"What do you think, Mr. Walker?" I looped my arm through his and pressed a quick kiss to his lips. He also looked stunning in a black suit and tie, his blond hair gelled into perfect, unruly spikes, and wearing his black-framed glasses that I found incredibly sexy. There was a large watch on his wrist and his signature silver rings on his fingers. He looked good enough to eat.

He grinned devilishly and whispered in my ear. "I think we need to ditch the party, Princess. That dress looks lush on you, but I imagine it would look even better on the floor."

"So naughty." I winked. "You're looking quite dapper tonight yourself. I may just take you up on that offer later, Reaper," I said, low enough for his ears only. He laughed, a deep, throaty sound that made my heart do flip flops in my chest.

The girls wore their black, lacy dresses, and Luther looked altogether miserable as he tugged on the bowtie he wore with his suit. A few other teenagers were milling around, who I recognized from Mac's school. Dressing in all black wasn't a stretch for most of her friends, but I was pleased that most of them had at least attempted to dress up for the occasion instead of wearing black jeans and T-shirts.

Grandma and Gus burst into the bar then, both looking decidedly un-goth. Grandma Betty wore the hot pink tracksuit she had spoken of on the phone, along with the white crocheted handbag she was never seen without. Gus wore his usual khaki Members Only jacket, sunglasses, and fedora hat. Mac spotted them coming in and scowled, no doubt disappointed that they clashed so spectacularly with her party's theme.

"Mac! There's my girl!" Grandma exclaimed, wrapping her arms around Mac in a suffocating embrace. She planted kisses on Mac's head, then held her out at arm's length to take a better look at her.

"Hi, Grandma," Mac said, glancing around to see if any of her friends had noticed the embarrassing moment.

Grandma put one hand to her mouth as she took in Mac's themed outfit and gasped. "You look so grown up in that dress, Mac! I didn't know you had cleavage already!"

Zeb stood behind me, his arms wrapped around my waist, and I felt his entire body shudder with silent laughter.

Mac turned to me, her eyes wide and mouth pursed in a thin line as if trying to send a telepathic message to me to save her.

She handed Mac a small pink box with a ribbon on top as I took Grandma by the elbow. "Your real gift isn't ready yet. This one will have to do for now!" she called to Mac as I steered her away.

With a chuckle, I showed Grandma and Gus to a booth in the corner where, hopefully, Grandma could keep her thoughts about Mac's cleavage to herself for the remainder of the party.

"Cricket, I still need to talk to you..." Grandma said, trailing off and giving Gus a side-eye to indicate to me that she didn't want to talk in front of him.

"I know. I'll take you out to lunch soon, okay?" I asked as she seated herself next to Gus, not waiting for her answer.

I turned to find Essie entering the bar... on the arm of Aiden Rhys, who I hated to admit, looked dashing in a black suit. My smile twisted into a scowl as I marched over to where they now stood, talking to Zeb.

"Cricket! Lovely party, everything looks perfect!" Essie exclaimed as she pulled me in for a cheek kiss. She looked gorgeous in a long, black fitted dress with sparkly fringe hanging from it in various places. She wore a headband with feathers attached, her long platinum blonde hair with chunky black highlights hanging loose. And, of course, her dark makeup was on point, as always. Her look was more "gothic flapper" than "Victorian gothic," but I thought Mac would be more than fine with it.

"Hi, babe, you look amazing!" I said, and as she kissed

my cheek. I whispered so that only she could hear me, "What's *he* doing here?"

She pulled back, giving me a quizzical look. "You remember Aiden, right? From our Girl's Night Out?"

I sighed and decided to try to make nice. Besides, this could be the perfect opportunity to learn more about him. "Of course, how could I forget the guy who crashed Girl's Night?" I asked, cocking my head at Aiden and smirking. Okay, so I would try to play nice after making that one snarky comment.

He and Zeb laughed, and Aiden glanced at Essie. "Can you really blame me? There was no way I was passing up the opportunity to meet this gorgeous woman," he drawled, looking at her appreciatively while her face went rosy under his stare. Barf.

The other guests trickled in two and three at a time, bearing gifts and hugging the birthday girl. When it appeared that everyone had arrived, I signaled to the waitress to start taking orders and bringing out drinks. Zeb had settled in at a table for four, along with Essie and Aiden, so I took my seat beside Zeb and plastered a fake smile on my face.

"So, Aiden, Cricket tells me you deal in antiques?" Zeb asked, taking a pull from his beer. He put one arm around me and pulled me close while waiting for Aiden's answer.

"Yeah, I do. 'Old shit,' right, Cricket?" Aiden asked with a chuckle, and Zeb laughed.

Essie reached for Aiden's hand with a huge grin on her face. "I've been showing him around Nashville. We've found quite a few amazing antique shops, haven't we?" she asked, her eyes bright as she turned to Aiden. I barely kept myself from rolling my eyes. Why did he evoke such a strong dislike from me? Maybe my Revealer senses were picking up on something that my brain wasn't. It was worth discussing with Zeb later, so I made a mental note to mention it to him.

Aiden smiled at her sweetly before turning back to us. "We have, but I still haven't found the piece my client is searching for, unfortunately." His mouth turned down in a small frown as he shrugged.

"Well, here's hoping it'll turn up soon, mate," Zeb said, raising his beer bottle in a toast before finishing it off.

Music started playing, and the guests started making their way to the dance floor. It was "Just Like Heaven" by The Cure, and Essie's eyes lit up when she recognized it. "I love this song! Come on, Aiden!" She grabbed his hand and pulled him to the dance floor.

Zeb and I sat in silence for a moment, watching Essie and Aiden laughing and dancing, along with almost everyone else. Mac and her friends had formed a circle and were dancing together. She actually looked happy for once, which made me happy.

"So, do you want to tell me what's going on, Princess?" Zeb asked. The waitress walked by, placing another beer in front of both of us just then. I immediately downed almost half of mine before answering.

I glanced at him. "What do you mean?"

Zeb actually rolled his eyes at me. "Your attitude about Aiden. It's obvious you don't like the bloke. Did he do or say something to you?" he asked, his tone quickly turning dark on that last part.

"No... I just don't trust him. Call it instinct or intuition, I don't know. He's up to something," I said, raising an eyebrow at Zeb over my beer.

Zeb bobbed his head. "Okay, I get that. A woman's intuition is a real thing, I'll grant you. But can you try, Cricket?

Let's give him a chance before we automatically assume he's up to no good."

I inhaled sharply. The truth was, I didn't understand my extreme reaction to him either unless it was the Revealer thing, so I couldn't really explain it to Zeb. "I'll try, alright? Maybe my supernatural radar detector is glitching." He grinned, grabbed my hand, and gave it a squeeze.

"Thank you. We'll keep an eye on him, but Essie just seems so happy. I like seeing her that way, you know?" he said, casting a sad smile in Essie's direction on the dance floor. I got the feeling there was more to the story behind that statement, but I decided now wasn't the time to go digging into her past.

I leaned into Zeb and he wrapped his arms around me. "Wanna dance, Princess?" he asked when the next song came on. I recognized it as "A Little Death to Laugh" by Cold Cave from Mac's playlists on our shared Spotify account.

The corner of my mouth turned up into a slow smile. "I thought you'd never ask." He stood and took my hand, leading me out onto the dance floor near Essie and Aiden. Essie smiled brightly at me. I was going to make an effort for Essie, I reminded myself and mustered up a grin.

We danced, eventually merging with Mac's circle of friends, all dancing together. Grandma Betty even joined us for a few songs, then said she should get back to Gus, who sat scowling in a corner booth. Mac and Regina flounced around in their vintage dresses, giggling and squealing when their favorite songs played. Luther looked as if he'd like to go home immediately, dancing stiffly and fidgeting with his bow tie often. The other guests seemed to be enjoying themselves—eating, drinking, and mingling.

I excused myself to use the bathroom, grateful for an excuse to catch my breath for a moment. Checking my hair and makeup in the mirror, I decided both looked a little worse for wear. I washed my hands, and headed back towards the source of the blaring music, almost tripping over my own feet when I noticed Aiden standing just outside the bathrooms, cell phone to his ear. I stopped just in time, without drawing his attention, and ducked back into the shadows.

You're supposed to be giving him the benefit of the doubt for Essie's sake, my inner voice of reason, who I called Logical Cricket, said to me. I mentally shrugged her off as my inner skeptic and all-around bad girl, Ho Cricket, spoke up. *See if you can hear what he's saying! He's up to no good, you know it!*

I did know it. In my gut, I knew something wasn't right about Aiden, even if I wasn't sure how I knew. I quietly drew as close as I could get without him seeing me. I crouched down in the shadows and listened.

"Not yet. But I'm getting closer. I understand how important it is." He paused, looking down at his feet, then back toward the guests. I could see his side profile, and I swore it looked as if he were staring directly in Mac and Regina's direction. I narrowed my eyes and waited for him to speak again as he began bobbing his head, silently agreeing with whatever the other party was saying.

"Yeah, yeah. Of course. I'm ninety-nine percent sure I know who has it." Another brief pause, then, "Don't worry about it. I'll get it, no matter what, okay?" The tone in his voice was disconcerting, even a little menacing. I could only assume he was referring to the artifact he said he was in town to find.

But who did he think had it?

I heard him saying his goodbyes and quickly ducked back into the restroom. I needed to think for a moment anyway, and he would be back on the dance floor with Essie by the time I left the bathroom.

Logical Cricket piped up again. *He said nothing incriminating. Just that he thought he knew who had the antique he's looking for.*

He is totally up to no good, Ho Cricket pointed out. I pushed them both into a mental coat closet and turned on the faucet, splashing my face with cold water and looking at myself in the mirror.

"Benefit of the doubt," I said aloud slowly, enunciating each word precisely to remind myself of my promise to Zeb.

I shouldn't have eavesdropped on Aiden. It had only made me more suspicious. I vowed to stick only to gathering the information Carl wanted about Aiden—his reasons for being in Nashville—and that was it. And as far as I was concerned, case closed. I knew he was here looking for an antique for a client, end of story. So, I decided to make an appointment to deliver my report to Carl first thing Monday evening and exited the restroom.

———

4

Monday night, I found myself sitting in a Formica chair inside Sunshine Cleaners, the dry cleaner that served as a front for the Ministry of Vampire Affairs. As I waited to see Carl, I once again took in the retro furnishings and design of the lobby. The place was a throwback to the 70s with its shag carpeting and the tattered sign out front showing a smiling sun holding a basket of laundry. After all this time, it still amazed me this place served as the headquarters for the largest chapter of the MVA in the country.

The receptionist was a pretty redheaded vampire named Alexandra. I'd met her on my very first visit with Carl when he prompted her to show me her fangs to prove vampires were indeed real. Alexandra had terrified me during that first meeting, but I'd interacted with her on many subsequent trips to Sunshine Cleaners to see Carl. I learned she was actually a very nice girl who just happened to have elongated canine teeth.

Alexandra pressed a button on her desktop phone after an annoying buzzing sound filled the room. She spoke briefly into her headset before turning to me. "Cricket, he'll see you now," she said with a charming smile.

"Thanks, Alex." I gathered my bag and headed in the direction of Carl's office.

I knocked at his door and waited until I heard Carl's Russian accented voice say, "Come." I opened the door, entering the only updated room in this entire building, as far as I knew.

Carl's office was all white. The desk, chairs, carpeting, you name it—stark white. Sleek, sexy, and immaculate. Entering his office always made me feel as if I needed to wash my hands before touching anything. He motioned to one of the guest chairs and said, "Sit," so I did.

"I assume you're here to give me an update on the dragon?" Carl asked. No "hello," no "how are you?" I should've been used to Carl's abrupt manner by now, but it still caught me off guard.

"You are correct." I crossed my legs and leaned back in the chair across from him. His large white desk separated us, with an open laptop and several file folders on it. He cocked his head at me and steepled his hands underneath his chin, waiting for me to go on.

I cleared my throat. "Well, his name is Aiden Rhys. He's an antique dealer from Atlanta, Georgia, and he's in town trying to locate an antique piece for one of his clients," I said, fidgeting with the hem of my shirt under Carl's steely gaze. "He said he was told there was a good chance he'd find it in Nashville, so he's been scouring the antique and thrift shops in the area. He hasn't found it yet, though."

Carl's expression remained unchanged. I'd felt so confident about giving Carl this update and washing my hands of Aiden Rhys. But after delivering that short and uninspiring report about the dragon shifter, I was anything but confident. It felt flimsy and weak like I'd barely done any research on Aiden. All of which was true. I'd promised Zeb to give Aiden a chance for Essie, and I'd translated that into not doing my job. My cheeks flushed as Carl stared at me as if waiting for more.

Finally realizing that was the end of my report, Carl took a deep breath and leaned back in his pristine white office chair. He leveled his whiskey-colored eyes at me, making me feel as if I was sixteen again and the principal was about to sentence me to detention.

"That's all you've uncovered on the dragon?" he asked, his accent thick and callous.

My breath caught in my throat. "I—yes, so far, I mean—" I stammered, feeling a slick sheen of sweat breaking out across my forehead. Would this be the night that a vampire finally drained me dry in a fit of rage due to my own ineptness? I sincerely hoped not.

He cocked his head at me, clasping his hands in front of him with his elbows propped up on the armrests of his chair. "What is the antique he's after? Who told him it would be in Nashville? Who is his client?" he asked, firing off all the questions I knew I should've had answers for. I bit my lip as I listened, mentally berating myself. "These are the questions we need answered, Cricket. I have to say, I'm disappointed in your work. Should I find someone else to investigate this dragon instead?"

I shook my head. "No, no. You're right. I'm sorry, Carl. I can do this. I let my emotions get in the way of doing my job, and it won't happen again. I promise." I placed one hand over my racing heart in the form of an oath.

Carl raised an eyebrow at me, no doubt wondering what "emotions" I was referring to, but he didn't ask, and I didn't elaborate. He stared at me silently for a few moments while

I bit my lip, waiting for a reply. Or for him to lunge at my neck, fangs bared.

"Do not disappoint me again, Cricket."

I exhaled a huge breath. "Thank you, Carl. I won't, I promise." Relief rushed over me. My pulse returned to normal as I gathered my crossbody bag, preparing to leave before he changed his mind about ripping my throat out.

"One more thing," he said, as my hand reached for the doorknob. I turned halfway, waiting for him to speak. "As I'm sure you know, dragon shifters can be devious, beguiling, and deceitful. Be on your guard around him. If this antique is important to Aiden, he will do *anything* to get it," Carl said.

I met his intense gaze briefly, then nodded before shutting the door behind me.

I SPENT the next few days in research mode, determined to make up for lost time with the Aiden Rhys case. I Googled him, stalked his Instagram, Facebook, and Twitter accounts, and even looked up public records on him in Atlanta. I turned up a bit more information—he worked for his family's high-end antique shop—Ignis Antiques— in Atlanta. He had a serious girlfriend for several years until about two years ago when she broke off the engagement. He'd been single and ready to mingle ever since, judging from the parade of fit, gorgeous women featured on his social media accounts. Aiden's family had money—old money—and lots of it. Also, he really loved taking selfies.

I'd spotted a few photos of Aiden and Essie together, in front of various Nashville antique shops or having lunch. She looked so happy in the photos, with her emerald eyes shining brightly and smiling so hard her cheeks probably ached. I hoped he wouldn't hurt her, but I feared he would.

I continued gathering tidbits of information on him and his family for the rest of the week while simultaneously dodging calls from Grandma. I owed her a visit to find out what she wanted to discuss with me, which I imagined was that she and Gus planned to elope in Vegas and head to Bermuda for the honeymoon. I liked Gus. He was a great guy despite the gruff exterior, but I wasn't so sure I was ready to hear about their impending nuptials, so I let her calls go to voicemail, and her texts remained unanswered.

By Friday night, I'd had about enough of Aiden Rhys, so I closed the laptop, which sat on the kitchen table, and decided to make dinner for Zeb. Mac usually ate vegan dinners at her boyfriend, Luther's house, or at Regina's, so I wasn't expecting her home for dinner. I dragged out the tin box full of index cards that contained handwritten recipes from my mom, Grandma Betty, and even a few from my great-grandmother. I settled on Chicken and Dumplings, one of Grandma Betty's, and set about making the dumplings from scratch while the chicken cooked in a pot on the stove.

As I worked, Mac burst into the kitchen, a scowl on her pretty face. Her perfectly plucked eyebrows were drawn together and her heavily smoked eyes blazed as she strode to the kitchen table and began turning over books, magazines, and bills.

"Mac, you're home early! Want me to make you a veggie burger?" I asked as she moved to the kitchen counter to continue her search.

"No thanks. I'm not hungry." She lifted the flour, sugar, and coffee canisters one by one, replacing them with a sigh.

"What are you looking for?" I asked as I finished rolling

out the dough. I picked up my paring knife and started cutting out bite-sized pieces for the dumplings.

"My ring. Have you seen it?" Mac asked with irritation, finally stopping to look at me.

I looked up and raised one eyebrow at her. "What ring? Did Luther pop the question, and you didn't tell me about it? If so, I need to have a conversation with that boy." I stabbed the dough with my knife as I waited for an answer.

She rolled her eyes and flipped a strand of her black hair over her shoulder. "No, Mom. It's the fake emerald ring Regina and I found in the trunk of old clothes we bought at the thrift store. I can't find it anywhere." She slumped into a chair at the kitchen table. As usual, she was dressed in hues of black and grey. She wore a black knit skirt with striped grey and white leggings underneath and a black hoodie featuring a unicorn skull surrounded by roses. She propped one elbow on the table and rested her chin on her fist, frowning.

I put the knife down and looked at her. "What's the big deal if it's fake? Order another one online." I checked on the chicken and returned to cutting out dumplings.

Mac pushed back from the table, standing up. "I knew you wouldn't understand. That ring is important to me, even if it is fake. God, Mom." She stomped out of the room, then I heard the front door slam.

Okay, then. I shrugged, wondering what was so special about that fake ring.

I finished cutting out the dumplings and added them to the boiling pot with the chicken. A delicious aroma filled the kitchen as I pulled a beer from the fridge and popped it open. The front door opened and there was Zeb standing in the doorway.

"Something smells absolutely ace, Princess," he said,

sniffing the air before wrapping an arm around me for a squeeze. I stood on my toes to give him a quick kiss, then offered him the beer I'd just opened, which he accepted eagerly.

"Chicken and dumplings, Grandma Betty's recipe," I said, retrieving another beer for myself from the fridge.

"Sounds great. I'm starved." He sat down at the table with his beer. I smiled as I turned my back to him, checking on the boiling pot of deliciousness on the stove.

When I turned around, Zeb had my laptop opened up, and the last website I visited was on the screen. It was a news article from a few years ago about Aiden Rhys. He looked up at me with a questioning gaze.

"What's this?" he asked, knowing good and well what it was. He scrolled the page, then clicked through a few more tabs that were still open, all of them showing Aiden's various social media accounts.

"Research," I said simply, sitting down at the table across from him, mildly annoyed that he opened my laptop up without asking. But I had nothing to hide from him, so I let it go.

"I thought you'd agreed to give Aiden a chance?" He slammed the laptop shut. His blue eyes simmered as he looked at me accusingly.

I pursed my lips as the blood rushed to my face in a flood of anger. "I did. But it so happens I have a job to do also, which requires me to find out what Aiden is doing in Nashville."

He shook his head. "He already told us, Cricket. Why can't you let it go?"

"He told us he's an antique dealer, and he's in town looking for a piece for his client. After agreeing to lay off Aiden, I took that information to Carl, hoping to be done with it. Obviously, he wasn't satisfied, so I need to find out more." I took a swig of my beer.

"So, you've been stalking his socials and spying on him?" Zeb asked, his eyes cold.

I blinked a few times in confusion. I cocked my head, staring back just as coldly. "Yes, though I prefer to call it 'research.' What's the big deal?"

"The 'big deal' is that Essie seems really happy lately, and it's got everything to do with Aiden. Why does Carl need to know what he's doing here? Does it really matter?" Zeb placed his empty beer bottle on the table.

"Have you forgotten the whole reason Carl hired me? Supernaturals are coming to Nashville in droves and a lone dragon shifter suddenly showing up here is something that needs to be checked into," I said, crossing my arms. "I have a job to do, Zeb. I don't tell you how to collect souls, so I'd appreciate the same courtesy."

He huffed, a snide smile on his face. "Okay, Cricket." I saw miniature flames sparking to life in his eyes when he looked my way. He was angry, and he wasn't the only one.

"You know what? Maybe you should find your own dinner tonight." I narrowed my eyes as he rose from the table.

"Maybe I should," he said, stomping out of the kitchen with one last glare at me.

"And don't open laptops that don't belong to you!" I called out right before I heard the front door slam. A hissing noise drew my attention to the stove where my chicken and dumplings were boiling over.

"Damn it!" I yelled to the empty house as I rushed to salvage my dinner.

TWO DAYS LATER, I headed to a cute little bistro downtown, where I had asked Essie to meet me for Sunday brunch. I had decided to talk to Essie and find out just how invested she was in Aiden. To hear Zeb tell it, she was ready to marry the guy, but I wasn't so sure. At least, I hoped she wasn't in that deep yet. I still had my suspicions about Aiden, even though I was trying my best to do my research with an open mind and only gather the facts for Carl. It was hard to ignore my gut feeling, especially since I was sure my Revealer senses were picking up on something my brain hadn't figured out yet.

I left Mac sleeping in her bed and locked the front door behind me as I headed out for my brunch date. I glanced at Zeb's door across the porch from mine. We hadn't spoken since Friday night, and I hadn't seen him either. Not even an apology text. Scowling at his door, I headed down the porch steps to my car. I had news for him; I would not be the one apologizing.

When I arrived at the bistro half an hour later, Essie waved to me from a table she'd already managed to get. The place was crowded. Sunday brunch was no joke around here. I smiled and made my way to her, savoring the bacon and maple-scented air as I did. My stomach growled loudly, and I was glad the noisy patrons were around to camouflage the sound.

"Cricket!" Essie exclaimed when I approached the table. She stood, grasped my arm and kissed my cheek. I hung my crossbody bag on the back of my chair before sitting down.

"How are you, Essie?" I asked, then noticed the mimosas in front of us. "Oh, thanks!" I added, lifting my drink to my lips as she laughed.

"How could we have brunch without mimosas, right?"

she asked, grinning as she took a sip from hers. "To answer your question, I'm great! What about you?"

She did seem great. Too great, as a matter of fact. Her long, black-streaked, platinum blonde hair was in a high ponytail, and she wore a short, white dress covered in tiny dark red flowers. A black leather jacket, black ribbon choker, and black boots completed her look, which was feminine but still retained the goth elements she and Mac were so fond of. Her clothing wasn't the issue. It was her demeanor that had changed.

Essie had never been this excited to see me before. I felt she simply tolerated me in the past for Zeb's sake, but anyone watching us now would think we were dear friends. She seemed almost giddy, and that was something Essie never was. Bold, fierce, sassy, and no-nonsense-Essie would never act like this. I raised an eyebrow as I contemplated how I wanted this conversation to go.

"I'm doing okay. You look amazing, by the way." I sipped my drink and savored the bubbly tartness. Mimosas were one of my favorite breakfast beverages, coming in a close second to coffee.

She beamed. "Thank you! I feel good too, you know? I haven't felt this way in a long time. You know how it is when you're falling for someone, right?" Her face flushed as her eyes seemed to stare right past me for a moment.

My stomach dropped. It appeared Zeb wasn't completely wrong; Essie did indeed have it bad for Aiden. I took a deep breath. Might as well get this over with.

"So, things are going well with Aiden, I take it?" I asked, starting slow. I'd have to play this by ear to find out what I could and hopefully not piss her off in the process.

She grinned from ear to ear, leaning in close. "Yes! Oh my God, Cricket. He's amazing. I can't believe how perfect he is. He is perfect, don't you think?" The waitress returned to take our orders thankfully, so I had a few moments to prepare an appropriate answer to her question.

When the waitress walked away, Essie was looking at me expectantly. Clearly, she wanted me to agree that Aiden was perfect in every way, but I couldn't do it in good conscience. I cleared my throat. "Perfect? What man is perfect?" I asked with a laugh, buying myself some time. I reached for my mimosa.

"Yeah, you're right. But he's pretty damn close, honestly, Cricket. He makes me feel like I'm the only woman in the world. He listens to me. He cares about what I think. He's not just interested in sex." She paused, then smiled slyly. "The sex is incredible too, though."

Oh, boy. I threw back the rest of my mimosa and waved to the waitress for another.

"But you've only known him for a couple of weeks. Maybe you should be cautious until you get to know more about him," I said, being careful with my words.

Essie frowned slightly as the waitress sat two more mimosas in front of us. "You were acting weird around him at the bar and at Mac's party. What's going on, Cricket? Do you know something about Aiden that I should know?" She crossed her arms in front of her, leaving her fresh drink untouched.

I ran a hand through my long blonde hair with a sigh. "My Revealer senses are telling me something isn't right about him. I don't know what it is yet, but I don't want you to get hurt, Essie." I gave her a half-smile, hoping that would smooth my words over a bit.

Apparently, it did not. She huffed, rolling her eyes. "Your Revealer senses? Maybe you're being a bit dramatic, yeah?

He's done nothing to earn your mistrust," she said, her emerald eyes narrowing as she spoke.

I didn't like how she said "Revealer senses" as if my abilities weren't real. Coming from a Grim Reaper, it would be laughable if it didn't piss me off so much.

"Well, did you know he was engaged until a couple years ago? Did he tell you his family is loaded? What about—"

Essie held up her hand. "Just stop. So what if he was engaged? Sometimes things don't work out. And what if his family has money, that's a bad thing? I just don't understand why you can't give him a chance," she said, her green eyes filled with disappointment. Our brunch plates arrived then, but neither of us made a move toward our food.

"I'm all for giving him a chance, Essie. I'm just saying, please keep your guard up. Be careful, okay?" I clasped my hands in front of me in a praying gesture.

She stared at me for a moment before relenting. "Okay, I'll be careful. If you'll promise to back off of him. Let him prove himself to me, one way or another, on his own, yeah?" Essie pulled her plate of syrup-soaked pancakes closer.

"I'll back off as much as I can while still doing my job for the MVA, alright?" I picked up a slice of bacon from my plate and took a bite.

"Deal." Essie grinned, and we ate our brunch in relative silence, each of us, no doubt, thinking about Aiden Rhys.

5

I arrived back home from brunch with Essie to find Zeb sitting on the glider on our shared front porch. I climbed the porch steps slowly, unsure what to expect from him. When I reached the top, I pursed my lips and paused, waiting for him to speak.

He patted the space next to him on the glider, so I made my way over and sat down, careful not to touch him. He took a drink from his beer, then offered it to me. I accepted, took a swig, and didn't give it back.

"I'm sorry, Princess."

"And?" I asked, taking another drink from what was now my beer. I wasn't going to make this easy for him.

"And I had no right to butt in and tell you how to do your job." I nodded, then waited for him to continue, which he did. "And I had no business looking at your laptop either," he added, then took my hand. "I'm sorry." He raised my hand to his lips and placed a gentle kiss on my knuckles.

A smile tugged at my lips while the butterflies in my stomach took flight. "Alright, you're forgiven, I suppose."

He grinned, his blue eyes sparkling. "Good. I hate it when you're pissed at me."

"Then stop doing things to piss me off," I said. He laughed and drew me into his muscular arms, my back resting against his chest.

After a few moments, I figured I'd better tell him about my brunch date before Essie did. Now that we'd made up, I didn't want him to get the wrong idea. "I just came from brunch with Essie."

"Yeah? How are things?" I knew that was code for "how mad is she?"

"She's good. She's crazy about Aiden," I said, pausing for a moment. Then I added, "I just asked her to be careful."

He gave me a squeeze and kissed the top of my head. I pushed off with my foot to rock us in the glider. "That's good," Zeb said simply.

I snuggled into him, taking another sip of beer and offering the last swallow to him, which he declined. I finished it off, and soon I fell asleep next to Zeb, who gently rocked us in the glider.

A FEW DAYS LATER, Mac, Regina, and I were watching HGTV in the living room after dinner when the doorbell rang. We were enjoying ice cream for dessert—theirs was vegan, mine was the regular fattening kind—and watching Chip and Joanna remodel a kitchen. With an irritated sigh, I sat my bowl of ice cream on the coffee table to see who dared come over without calling first.

I swung the door open to find Grandma Betty.

"Cricket! Why haven't you been answering my phone calls?" she asked, barging into the living room. She wore a purple knee-length dress, white sandals, and of course, her white crocheted handbag dangled from one arm. Her silver hair was arranged in a stiff helmet of curls and hairspray, while her large rose gold glasses rested on her nose.

"Please, come in," I said sarcastically, as she'd already made herself at home on the couch next to Mac. I closed the door and dropped back into the recliner with my ice cream, hoping she wouldn't stay long.

"Hi, Grandma," Mac said as Grandma pulled her close for a hug.

"Hi," Regina said quietly, giving Grandma a shy smile.

"At least the two of you are happy to see me!" Grandma said, shooting me a look full of daggers. I rolled my eyes and stuck a spoonful of ice cream in my mouth before I said something I'd regret.

"Mac, do you remember at your party when I said your real gift wasn't ready yet?" she asked.

Mac's eyes went wide as she turned to face Grandma. "Yes..." she said. Her eyes darted to me, and I shrugged.

"Well, why don't you take a look outside?" Grandma asked, giving Mac a wink. The girls looked at one another, then jumped up from the couch to look out the window.

Oh, no.

Mac screamed. Regina screamed. They both screamed while holding each other's hands, jumping up and down.

I looked at Grandma, who smiled sweetly. "What the hell did you do?" I put my ice cream down again to go investigate what had prompted such a response. Grandma didn't answer, just continued to grin.

I pulled the curtains back. What appeared to be a brand new, black Volkswagen Beetle sat in our driveway, sparkling in the fading sun.

I let the curtain drop and turned back to Grandma. "Are you insane?"

"Thank you, Grandma! I love it!" Mac exclaimed, running to throw her arms around Grandma Betty. She dug some keys out of her handbag and dangled them in front of Mac, who took them and rushed out the door with Regina in tow.

"You didn't answer me. Are you crazy? What's the matter with you? She just turned sixteen, and you're giving her a brand new car?" I threw my hands up in the air, exasperated. "You could have asked me first, you know."

Grandma glared at me. "I could have if you would answer your phone. I don't know what's gotten into you lately, Cricket. You still haven't taken me out for lunch so we can talk." She crossed her arms across her chest and turned her head away from me, pouting like a child.

"The car is going back. You can't give her a CAR, Grandma." I ignored the part about me not answering my phone or taking her to lunch. She had a point, but I didn't feel like acknowledging it right now.

"You saw how happy it made her. Do you really want to tell her she can't have it?" she asked, knowing good and well what my answer would be.

I marched to the window and drew the curtain back again. Mac and Regina were inside the running car, the headlights on and music blaring so loudly I could hear the bass from where I stood. They were grinning from ear to ear, no doubt imagining all the places they could go in Mac's new car.

I groaned. "Fine. She can keep it, but there will be ground rules," I said through gritted teeth, watching them.

"Of course, dear," Grandma said, humoring me now.

"I can't believe you." I threw myself back into the

recliner. I picked up my ice cream and angrily put the spoon in my mouth.

"While I'm here, maybe we can have that talk?" She looked pleased with how this had all turned out. She'd given Mac an exorbitant gift and had earned Mac's eternal gratitude, pissed me off, and had cornered me into having this big secret discussion with her, too. *Bravo, Grandma.*

I was about to say something she probably wouldn't have liked about where she could go and who she could talk to when the girls burst back into the house.

"Grandma, can we drive you home? I have my learner's permit," Mac asked Grandma, then turned to me with pleading eyes. "Please, Mom? You have to come too, so there's an adult in the car after we drop Grandma off." She bounced up and down, hands clasped in front of her, her eyes begging me to say yes.

I sighed. It was nice to see her so happy, I had to admit. She'd been sullen and withdrawn ever since John-Clarke left town, blaming me for everything. Maybe this would be my chance to redeem myself—just a little in her eyes.

"Okay, let's go," I said, which prompted more screams and laughter from the girls. I turned to Grandma, who frowned.

"Guess that talk is going to have to wait," I said to her with a smirk, rising from the recliner to take my half-eaten bowl of ice cream to the kitchen.

ON SATURDAY NIGHT, I strode into the living room where Zeb waited for our date.

"Wow! Looking gorgeous, Princess," Zeb said with a low whistle. I shot him a smoldering glance and struck a pose, then stuck my tongue out at him. I had to admit, though, I thought I looked pretty damn good myself. My long blonde hair loose, my lips red, and a curve-hugging black mini dress with black pumps completed my look. I had even traded in my trusty crossbody bag for a little black clutch covered in sequins. I felt like a million bucks.

Until I remembered the details of our date. We had agreed—actually, Zeb had decided on our behalf—to a double-date with Essie and Aiden tonight. I hadn't been pleased when he'd told me, but I'd decided to bite my tongue and make the best of it. Besides, maybe it would be an opportunity to learn more about Aiden and what he was looking for. Plus, they wanted to go to a fancy restaurant in downtown Nashville, which gave me an excuse to get dressed up.

Zeb looked dashing as well in a black suit and tie, silver rings, and the tattoos on the backs of his hands peeking out from his sleeves. He stood and pulled me close, kissing me softly and probably smearing my red lipstick, but I didn't care. I grabbed his tie and continued the kiss, my heart racing.

"Are y'all going to a funeral or something?" Mac asked, walking into the living room with a bowl of soup. She sat down and immediately started flipping channels on the television, stopping when she reached HGTV.

Zeb barked a laugh, and I swatted his arm. A double-date with Aiden could be considered a funeral, I felt like saying. But I didn't. Instead, I said, "You're one to talk, Goth Queen. Everything you own is black," as I grabbed my coat.

"Don't do anything I wouldn't do," she called as we closed the door behind us.

We got into my car, which was parked next to Mac's new car, and I sighed. I'd taken her to get her permanent driver's license a few days before and had also laid a few ground rules: no driving at night by herself, no more than one friend in the car with her, no messing with the radio or her phone while driving. And many other rules that I couldn't remember right now. She had agreed to all of them, and so far, Mac and Grandma were happy. I wished I was.

I was still irritated with Grandma for buying my barely sixteen-year-old daughter a brand new car without consulting me. So what if I wasn't answering her calls? She should've waited to talk to me. I got worked up about it all over again, and Zeb must have noticed it, too.

"Alright, Cricket? Something bothering you?" he asked as he pulled my car out of the driveway, one hand on my thigh. He gave it a squeeze and glanced at me quickly before turning his attention back to the road.

"Sorry, it's Mac's car. I still can't believe Grandma did that." I shook my head. "I'll try to stop thinking about it."

"It was a nice gesture, although she went about it the wrong way." After a moment, he added, "I thought you might be upset about seeing Aiden tonight." He shot me a quick glance.

"I can't say I'm looking forward to it, but I'm making an effort." I put my hand on the back of his neck, massaging it a bit until he let out a groan.

"If you keep doing that, I'll have to turn this car around, Princess," he said, leaning into my touch.

I laughed. "Don't tempt me."

We reached the restaurant and let the valet park the car. *Fancy.* Aiden and Essie were inside at the spacious bar, already having a drink. Essie rushed over to me, kissing me on the cheek, as had become her customary greeting, and gave Zeb a quick hug. Her black-streaked platinum hair was pulled up into a messy, but elegant, updo and wore a tight-fitting emerald green dress that matched her eyes. Her gothic makeup was on point as she beamed at us.

"I'm so glad you're here! Isn't this place the best?" she asked, looking around. It was enormous, with dimmed lighting and a wall laden with all sorts of liquor bottles behind the bar. Aiden stood and put an arm around Essie's waist, smiling at us, looking dapper in his black suit paired with an emerald green tie, which matched Essie's dress. It was all I could do to control the scowl that threatened to erupt on my face.

"Thanks for joining us. How are you, Cricket?" he asked me.

I raised an eyebrow at being singled out but decided to play nice. "Couldn't be better, and you?"

He laughed, glancing at Essie, who stared at him adoringly. I almost wanted to vomit.

Aiden's name was called before he could reply, and soon we were seated at a table with a black leather U-shaped bench seat surrounding it. The lighting was dim here too, soft music played in the background, and although the dining area was crowded, it wasn't noisy. The waiter took our orders and brought back some appetizers and wine.

Zeb put his arm around me, and I leaned into him, taking a sip of my wine. I started to relax, letting the worries about Mac, her new car, Grandma, and Aiden fall away. Zeb and I were going to have a good evening with good food and good friends. *Well, one of them was a good friend, anyway.*

Essie leaned into Aiden's embrace, similar to how I was sitting with Zeb. She laughed at all his jokes, hung on every word he said. It was nauseating, to be honest, but I kept quiet and laughed when I was supposed to and kept drinking wine.

I felt rather buzzed when both Zeb's and Essie's phones

chirped at the same time. They looked at each other, then at their phones.

"Damn," Zeb said, rubbing his beard stubble while reading the text.

"Oh, no," Essie added, shooting an apologetic glance at Aiden. "Duty calls, babe."

"What?" I nearly spit out my wine.

"We have to go, Princess. Ten car pile-up in West Nashville. We're needed," he said, giving me a look and kissing my forehead. Since he and Essie were both Grim Reapers, working for Death Inc., the accident must have been bad if they were both called in. He went to scoot out of the booth, and Essie followed suit.

"Okay, I guess we'll have to call it a night then," I said, scooting my way out of the booth, too.

Zeb stopped me. "Why don't the two of you stay? Dinner hasn't even been served yet. You can get to know each other better, enjoy your meal, and bring mine home in a doggy bag for later." He winked. I glared at him, my jaw dropping.

Essie beamed. "That's a great idea, Sebby!"

I turned to Aiden for his reaction, and he looked as if Zeb had just suggested that Aiden stick his arm into a tank full of piranhas.

"Oh, I don't know..." I said, trailing off.

"Yeah, Cricket probably has things to do," Aiden added, clearing his throat and adjusting his tie.

"Don't be silly," Zeb said, giving me a squeeze and a kiss on the cheek, preparing to leave. If looks could have killed, Essie would have been tasked with collecting *his* soul right now from the glare I was sending his way.

"It's settled then! You two have fun. I can't wait to hear all about it!" Essie exclaimed, giving me a little wave. "Sebby,

I'll drive us so Cricket can drop Aiden off before she goes home, yeah?"

"Perfect," I grumbled.

And they were off.

And I was alone with Aiden.

6

W e made awkward small talk and drank lots of wine while we waited for dinner to be served. We ate in near silence, only commenting on how good the food was, both declining dessert in our mutual desire to get the hell out of there as fast as possible. As we waited on the check, Aiden leveled his gaze at me, placing his napkin on the table.

"Cricket, I think we've had enough wine tonight for us to be honest here. Tell me why you don't like me." He cocked his head to the side and waited for my answer.

I thought for a moment. I had definitely had a lot of wine and should really sit here for a while before I tried to drive, anyway. I needed to get some information out of him, and if he was in the mood for a heart-to-heart, why not?

"I know what you are, Aiden." I cut right to the chase.

He laughed nervously, looking around. "What do you mean?"

I rolled my eyes. "You're a dragon shifter. I know, so you can drop the act."

His eyes widened. He glanced around the restaurant

furiously, then scooted around the U-shaped bench seat and closer to me.

"Who are you? Or should I be asking—what are you?" he asked. I picked up the smoky tang of metal in his aura, just like I had the first time I'd met him.

I didn't see the harm in telling him at this point, so I did. "I'm a Revealer. A supernatural radar detector, to put it plainly, and the first time I met you, I knew." I downed the last of my wine. "As for why I don't like you... I can't answer that. It's almost as if my Revealer senses don't like you, not me. Why don't YOU tell ME why?"

He scoffed, looking away. "That makes no sense. I told you why I'm here, me being a—" he paused, lowering his voice, "—dragon shifter has nothing to do with anything." Even through my alcohol-induced haze, I sensed his aura growing stronger, the sharp metallic scent permeating the surrounding air.

A silent alarm went off inside of me, flashing "DANGER!" as I watched him. This was new; were my Revealer senses evolving? How could it know he was lying when my brain didn't? This was all very confusing, and my intoxicated condition wasn't helping matters.

"You're lying." The words boldly escaped my mouth before I could stop them. I leaned back, watching him squirm.

"I don't know what you're talking about, but I will not sit here and let you call me a liar. I'll find my own way back to Essie's place," he growled, throwing a few bills on top of his empty plate and pushed back from the table.

"Listen to me. If you hurt Essie or anyone else important to me for that matter, you will regret it." I grabbed his wrist. The tingling sensation I picked up from him the first time we met was there now, but I didn't let it distract me. "Do I need to remind you who you're dealing with? Surely you've figured out what Zeb and Essie are by now."

His gaze was fixed on my hand, which was still wrapped around his arm. He shook me off, then leveled his icy stare at me. "I do know. It seems you're the one who doesn't realize who you're dealing with here." He gave me a wicked smile that didn't quite reach his eyes. "If I don't find what I'm looking for soon, I won't be the only dragon in town—that's what you should be worrying about, Cricket."

And with that, Aiden strode out of the restaurant, leaving me speechless.

"SHUG, did you see this jacket? I have to have it!" Doreen exclaimed, holding up the most hideous, bejeweled denim jacket I'd ever seen in my life. She turned it back and forth, letting the light hit each gemstone, grinning from ear to ear.

"Wow, that's... really something, Doreen," I said, amused. I cringed as she clutched the garment to her chest and took off in the direction of the cash register.

Doreen and I had been hitting up every thrift store and antique shop we could find in the Nashville area for the past couple of days. I decided that I needed to figure out what Aiden was looking for and find it before he did. I figured he had probably visited most of these shops already and had most likely described the item to them in detail. In fact, I was counting on it.

I spotted a clerk, so I headed her way. "Excuse me, can you tell me if this man has been in your store recently?" I asked as I approached her, holding my cell phone out for her to see. I had Aiden's Facebook profile photo pulled up on the screen, his irritatingly handsome face staring at the store employee.

Her face wrinkled up in confusion, before moving her gaze to my phone. "No, I don't think so," she said, dismissing me.

"Are you sure? It's important."

"Mom?" I heard a familiar voice behind me. The clerk simply shrugged and continued with her work while I spun around to find Mac and Regina. They looked from me to Doreen, who had just finished paying for her bedazzled denim jacket, quizzical expressions on their faces.

"Mac? What are you doing here?" I asked, still holding my phone out. Mac glanced at it, her eyes widening.

"Why is there a picture of Essie's boyfriend on your phone? What are you doing, Mom?" she asked, crossing her arms and popping one hip out. Regina followed suit, on pure principle, I guessed.

"Oh, I—" I stammered, quickly stuffing my phone into my crossbody bag. *Crap, what now?*

Doreen approached and spoke before I had a chance to come up with a plausible lie. "We've been visiting all the shops around here, trying to find out if Aiden has been to them and if he bought anything." I turned to stare at her, open-mouthed. Well, so much for coming up with a good lie.

"Do you mind?" I asked incredulously. She shrugged.

Mac pulled a face, then said, "Why?"

Sighing, I said, "Because he's looking for an antique for his client. And my boss wants to know what it is and why they want it. Are you happy now?" My gaze drifted over the three of them, lingering on Doreen as she flushed.

"Well, you could've just asked us. We've been to almost every thrift shop in Middle Tennessee," Regina piped up, glancing at Mac for confirmation, her face lighting up. Regina and Mac shared the same taste in almost everything, including music, makeup, and clothing. They both wore black jeans, vintage band T-shirts, and smokey eyes. Regina's dark skin and long, dark curly hair contrasted with Mac's pale skin and long straight black hair, but their styles were identical.

"That's true. And if you really want to know, we saw him at a shop recently," Mac said, then walked away from me and toward a rack filled with black jackets.

I scrambled to follow. "Wait, what? Where? What did he buy?" I asked in rapid succession, trailing behind her. Doreen and Regina followed in my wake.

"Oh my God, Regina, this would look so good on you," Mac said, ignoring me and holding up a long black trench coat for Regina's appraisal.

"Mac!" I exclaimed, throwing my arms up in the air.

"God, Mom. Chill." She rolled her eyes at me and curled up her dark red lips in a smirk.

I took a deep breath and told myself strangling her wouldn't be worth the prison time. I doubted they served my brand of coffee in there, anyway. "Just tell me," I said through gritted teeth.

"Fine. There's an antique shop on Clinton Street. We saw him there a few weeks ago," Mac stated, still looking through the racks.

"That's where we bought the trunk full of clothes and costume jewelry," Regina added, admiring the trench coat Mac had found.

"Okay, well, did he see you? Did you talk to him?" I asked. My recently acquired Revealer alarm was going off again inside of me. Had Aiden threatened the girls?

"No, I don't think he saw us. When we saw him with

Essie at my party, we recognized him from the shop," Mac said, moving to another rack with me in tow.

"Did you happen to notice if he bought anything? Or overhear any conversations he had with the clerk?" I asked, pumping her for as much information as I could. At least he hadn't noticed the girls. That was a relief.

"Don't remember. At the time, we didn't even know him, you know? Are you done?" she asked, raising an eyebrow at me.

I pouted. "I guess. Are you driving?" I switched topics, still feeling cranky about Grandma and Mac's new car.

She rolled her eyes again. "Yes, Mom. I'm being super careful."

"She is, Mrs. Jones," Regina agreed, nodding her head at me.

"Alright. See you at home later?" I asked, turning away to find Doreen. As I did, I noticed a flash of green on Mac's finger as she held up yet another black garment for inspection.

"Yeah, I guess," she said absently, flipping the dress over.

"You found your ring?" I asked, nodding to her finger when she looked up.

She glanced at the ring and smiled brightly. "Yep, I found it under my pillow, isn't that strange? I guess I looked everywhere in my room except there." She shrugged and smiled again before turning back to the racks of vintage clothing.

Strange indeed.

Doreen and I went to the antique shop on Clinton Street to find it already closed for the day, so I headed home and made plans to revisit it soon. It was dusk as I pulled into the driveway and noticed Mac's car was still gone. I parked next to Zeb's bike; I hadn't spoken to him since the night he and Essie had abandoned me with Aiden at the restaurant. It wasn't intentional—our schedules just hadn't allowed for it. However, I was still pissed about it, even though Zeb and Essie couldn't have helped being called away for work.

As I was getting out of the car, Zeb's front door opened. He came out and stood on the porch, watching me walk up the drive with a half-cocked grin on his face. He looked hot as hell in a tight gray T-shirt that showed off his tattooed muscles and ripped black jeans that hugged his thighs.

"Avoiding me, Princess?" he asked with a wink. I smiled, rolling my eyes as I tossed my bag to land next to my front door. He shoved his hands in his pockets and waited for my reply, and I realized maybe he did think I had been avoiding him.

"Of course not. I've been busy with work, and I thought you were too." I sauntered over to him, wrapping my arms around him and taking in his scent of leather and sandalwood. He hugged me back and planted a kiss on top of my head.

"So, you're not mad about the other night then?" he asked, tentatively.

I laughed. "Oh, I'm mad. Pissed, actually. You need to make it up to me," I teased, although it was somewhat true.

"Is that so? I reckon I can do that... got any suggestions?" He chuckled.

"I have so many suggestions. In fact, I'd like to share a few of them with you." I leaned my head back while still in his arms so I could meet his gaze. His eyes darkened with desire as one eyebrow shot up.

"Mrs. Jones, are you propositioning me?" he asked, acting scandalized.

I shot him a devious grin. "Yes. Yes, I am," I admitted, biting my lip.

"You don't have to ask me twice." He swept me off my feet and into his arms as he kicked in the partially open door, carrying me inside his half of the duplex we shared. I let out a little shriek, laughing as he placed me on the couch.

My giggles faded as his mouth crashed into mine, his body hovering above me as I laid on his couch. I kissed him back, my tongue slipping between his lips. He caught my lower lip with his teeth and gave it a nip, sending a bolt of electricity directly to my core. Zeb began making his way south, kissing a blazing trail down my neck and collarbone while his hands explored my body, roaming underneath my shirt, stroking my breasts.

My hands skimmed over his muscled arms and down his back. I let out a soft moan as he balled the fabric of my shirt in his fist, pulling it up over my breasts, kissing my stomach and chest. I raised up a bit and quickly discarded my shirt and bra while he pulled the T-shirt he wore over his head and shed his jeans and underwear, throwing them in a heap on the floor.

Zeb growled as his tongue found one of my nipples, teasing and licking while his hands drifted down my hips, tracing over my thighs. My back arched as he continued, moving to my other breast. Heat flooded through me, the familiar tingling, swirly sensation settling deep in my belly. He smiled against me, his breath warm on my skin. My fingers threaded through his spiky blond hair as he continued kissing his way down my body, so painfully slow.

"How am I doing, Princess? Have I made it up to you

yet?" he whispered, licking and sucking, his tongue burning a path across my skin as his hands worked the button on my jeans, finally ridding me of them.

I moaned when his fingers brushed over the damp cotton fabric of my panties, just over my core. "Not yet, keep going," I said breathlessly.

A throaty laugh escaped him while he removed my panties and stroked me. My breath hitched, my hips bucking against his hand when he pushed one finger deep inside. Stroke after stroke, then another finger, dipping in and out while his thumb massaged my sensitive spot. I moved against him, meeting each delicious thrust.

My blood felt like molten lava pumping through my veins when Zeb removed his hand and poised his hard length at my entrance. I lifted my hips to meet him as he thrust into me, filling me entirely. We moved in perfect synch, the constant retreat and return hitting just the right spot within me.

I raked my nails down his back, all the way to his ass. His muscles flexed with every thrust. "Zeb..." I moaned, his name sounding like a plea, a curse, and a prayer all at once.

Zeb dipped his head toward mine, his lips claiming a fierce kiss as he pressed into me. My body was on fire, so consumed by the heat and pressure building inside with every movement of our bodies.

"God, you feel so good," he groaned as I wrapped my legs around him. He picked up the pace, and a few more thrusts sent both of us over the edge. He pulled out, finishing as he did, and collapsed on top of me, our sweaty bodies tangled together. Zeb reached down for his discarded T-shirt, wiping me clean as we each tried to catch our breath. He rested his head on my breasts, his thumb gently stroking my hip.

My fingers combed through his hair while we recovered. I closed my eyes, my pulse slowing, my blood cooling, and my body relaxing.

"Consider yourself forgiven, Reaper," I said breathlessly. Zeb's body shuddered against mine with silent laughter as I drifted off to sleep.

7

The doorbell rang Friday afternoon while I was busy stalking Aiden's social media again. There was nothing particularly interesting; more selfies, more shots of Essie staring at Aiden as if he had hung the moon, and more images of what Aiden had to eat at every restaurant he visited. Boring, and no help at all.

I slammed my laptop shut and answered the front door. I was taken aback to see who was standing on my porch. "Regina!" I exclaimed, surprised to see her here without Mac, wherever Mac was.

Zeb and I met Regina months ago, when my first vampire boss, Nina, had forced me to help her find a reversal for a curse that had been put on her. Regina was a witch and helped us track down the cure, which, unfortunately for Nina, came too late to save her. After the dust had settled, Zeb and I thought that since Regina was around Mac's age, they might hit it off since they had so much in common. We were right; the two had been virtually inseparable since. We made it clear to Regina that she couldn't spill the supernatural beans to Mac, and so far, so good. Mac seemed to be a lot happier after making friends with Regina, which made me happy, too.

"Hi, Mrs. Jones," she said, wringing her hands. She peered around me, then met my gaze again. "Mac's not home, is she? I didn't see her car in the driveway." Her perfect brows drew together as she frowned, waiting for my response.

Regina was a year older than Mac, a pretty girl with dark skin, long, curly black hair, and piercing green eyes. She shared Mac's affinity for all things goth, including black clothing, smoky eyes, and black lipstick. They were like two peas in a pod.

I opened the door up wider, allowing her inside. "No, she's not here. Which begs the question, why are you?"

She came inside and sat on one end of the L-shaped couch, twirling a ring on her index finger. "I'm sorry to bother you. I just don't know what else to do." She bit her lip and shook her head.

"What's up?" I asked, sitting in the recliner facing her. I leaned forward; she had my attention, and I was beginning to worry.

She closed her eyes briefly, then exhaled. "I'm not sure if I should tell you any of this. Maybe it's nothing," she said with a shrug, her distressed gaze meeting mine.

"Is she pregnant?" I squinted at her.

"No! Nothing like that," Regina said, shaking her head, a smile tugging at her mouth despite her worried state. "It's not really anything, honestly, but I thought maybe it *could* turn into something... so I figured I should let you know and—"

I held up a hand. "Regina, just say it already," I said impatiently. Was something wrong with Mac? Was she keeping something from me? Every worst-case scenario started running through my mind, and my nerves couldn't take Regina's waffling.

"Okay, I'm sorry," she said, then took a deep breath. "Mac has seemed... different... since we found that trunk full of vintage clothes and stuff. Have you noticed anything?" Regina searched my face as she spoke.

I thought for a few moments before answering. I'd noticed a few things that were out of the ordinary, but nothing that had alarmed me. I remembered her searching the house frantically for the fake emerald ring she'd lost the other day. That was a little strange.

"Nothing much," I replied. She frowned. "Why, what's going on?"

"So, when we were in the shop on Clinton Street, where we found the trunk, that's when I first noticed it. It's like she was drawn to the trunk full of clothes and fake jewelry. She never left it once she spotted it. She insisted on buying it, although there didn't seem to be that much in it I liked." She wrinkled her brows again. "She got furious at me when I said we shouldn't bother with it. So I gave in, and we split the cost and brought it back to my house." She shrugged.

"Well, what did you all find inside the trunk, besides the dresses and the ring she's been wearing lately?" I cocked my head. Maybe Mac had spotted something inside the trunk that she really liked or thought was valuable, and that's why she had insisted on buying it.

"That's it, really. A few old dresses, some jewelry, and some old books," Regina said, twirling the ring on her finger again. "She put on that ring and refused to take it off. And from then on, she seemed... different." Regina shrugged, seemingly at a loss for words.

"You keep saying 'different,' but what do you mean?" I felt an odd sensation in the pit of my stomach. I knew exactly what Regina meant, and that's what scared me. Subtle differences. Things that were easily overlooked, but when you really thought about it, you knew something was different. You just couldn't put your finger on what. That's what Regina meant, and I'd noticed it, too.

"I don't know. It's hard to explain. Did she tell you she broke up with Luther?"

My jaw dropped. "Nooooo. She didn't. What happened?" I asked, not able to help myself. Mac dumping Luther was huge. So why the hell didn't I know about it already?

Regina's eyes went wide. "That's just it. She just told him out of the blue that they should see other people for no apparent reason. It devastated Luther." She frowned.

I shook my head in disbelief. "Are you sure? They've been together since sixth grade."

"I'm sure. I don't know what's going on, Mrs. Jones. And before you ask, no, I haven't told her about anything or shown her my powers. I wouldn't break my promise to you and Mr. Walker." She looked so earnest I had to believe her.

"Alright," I said, pronouncing the word slowly while I processed. "Thank you for coming to me, Regina. Please, call or text me if you notice anything else I should be aware of."

Regina frowned but nodded.

"Hey, you're a good friend to Mac. You care about her. That's why you're here. Don't feel bad, okay?" We stood, and I gave Regina a quick hug. She smiled when I released her, then turned to me as she stood at the door.

"Do you think it could be the ring?" she asked, one hand on the doorknob. "She hasn't let me get close enough to it to find out, so I'm not sure."

I raised an eyebrow. "I don't know, but maybe I can find out." She nodded, then closed the front door behind her when she left. I dropped back onto the couch, putting my head in my hands and wondering what the hell was going on with my daughter.

THE NEXT DAY, I finally decided to visit Grandma and find out what burning secret she was dying to discuss with me. I was dreading it, sure it was going to be about her and Gus getting married, but I supposed I had put off the inevitable long enough. If they wanted to get married, they would get married, with or without my support.

Mac came home late last night, long after Regina's visit and long after dark. One of the rules surrounding her new status as a vehicle owner was that she wasn't allowed to drive after dark. We argued about it when she got home. That had resulted in her being grounded from her car for the rest of the weekend. She stomped upstairs, slammed her door, and blasted some dark and gloomy music until the wee hours of the morning. That had resulted in me getting little sleep, which was why I was pouring my third cup of coffee into a travel mug as I prepared to go see Grandma and Gus.

Mac was still in her room, presumably asleep, so I opened her bedroom door softly to check on her before leaving. She was in bed, an old quilt Grandma Betty had made pulled up over her head. My inner troublemaker wanted to spitefully jerk the covers off of her and tell her to wake up in retaliation for being kept awake last night with her music. But my mother's instinct kicked in, and I thought better of it.

I crept a little closer to her bed and whispered, "Mac? Are you awake? I'm heading over to Grandma Betty's. Do you want to go with me?" I paused, waiting for a grunt, a groan, or a pillow to fly in my direction. None came, so I figured she was out cold and closed the door behind me as I left.

About thirty minutes later, I stood in front of Grandma's door inside Forever Young. I knocked and waited, nodding and smiling at a nurse as she hurried down the corridor to another apartment. Finally, Gus jerked the door open with a scowl.

"Cricket, what are you doing here?" he asked. His white hair was sticking up in all directions, similar to a troll doll's, and he wore a navy bathrobe, cinched at the waist. He appeared to have nothing on underneath, and I averted my gaze quickly before seeing something traumatizing.

"Gus!" I cried, shielding my eyes with one hand and turning away. "You're naked!" I half-whispered and half-screamed, cringing and continuing to not look at him.

"For God's sake, I'm wearing boxers under here," he said, throwing his hands up in the air. I risked a peek at him through my fingers and saw that, indeed, no bits were showing through the slit of his robe.

With a sigh of relief, I put my hands down and met his gaze. Even in this state of undress, Gus still wore his dark sunglasses, but I was used to it by now. His brows furrowed, disappearing behind his glasses.

"Again, I'll ask. What are you doing here?" I felt him glaring at me from behind the glasses.

"I came to see Grandma. She's been after me to come to visit," I explained, trying to peek around him into the apartment. "Can I come in?"

With a heavy sigh, Gus opened the door just enough to allow me through. I stepped into the living room of the small apartment and gasped. The place was a mess. A pizza box and empty bottles of beer littered the coffee table. Grandma's afghans were strewn haphazardly across the couch and recliner, not neatly folded on the back of the couch like they usually were. I looked across the open space into the kitchen area and saw the sink full of dishes and dirty pots and pans on top of the stove. I turned in disbelief to look at Gus, who stood smoking a cigar right behind me.

"What's going on?" I asked him, eyes narrowed. Grandma would never allow any of this to happen on her watch, so either she wasn't here and hadn't been for some time, or she'd finally gone senile. I was betting on the former. "Where's Grandma?"

With a huff, Gus sat heavily on the couch, so I moved a pair of discarded pants with the tips of my fingers and sat down on the recliner across from him.

"I don't know, Cricket," he said despondently, putting his head in his hands. I watched the cigar precariously held between his fingers, wishing he'd set it down somewhere.

I shook my head. "What do you mean, you 'don't know?' When did you see her last?"

"A couple of nights ago. She took a bag with a few of her things and left, didn't say where she was going," he said, voice shaky and weak.

I rubbed my face, letting my hands rest on my cheeks. "Okay, well, did you two fight? What happened?"

"No! That's the thing. Nothing happened. She turned off the television while I was watching a game and said she 'couldn't take it anymore' and walked out." He shrugged and dragged one hand through his white troll hair.

I stood up and looked around the room as if she would just pop out from behind a door. "Gus, why didn't you call me?" I turned to face Gus, who frowned.

"I thought she was going to your place. Why would I call

you?" he asked, shrugging. He had a point. It was logical to think that Grandma would show up at the duplex, but she hadn't. So, where on earth could she be?

I sighed. "Alright, tell me the apartment numbers of her friends. I'll check with them. She's not at my place, so she has to be around here somewhere." I dug my phone out of my purse. I looked at the screen; no missed calls from Grandma. However, there was a missed call from Zeb, but I'd call him back later.

Gus recited several apartment numbers and names to me, which I hurriedly made a note of in my phone, then I left him to drown his sorrows in alcohol, with a reminder to have the place cleaned up by the time Grandma came back.

AFTER VISITING a half dozen apartments in Forever Young, I still hadn't found Grandma. I decided to head back home and make some calls. Hopefully, I'd be able to track her down somewhere. But when I pulled into the driveway at the duplex, I saw Grandma's car parked next to Zeb's bike, in the spot where Mac's car should have been. I'd have to deal with Mac later, though. I needed to find out what was going on with Grandma and Gus.

Zeb was on the porch waiting for me, a pinched look on his face. He was wearing his favorite flannel shirt, jeans, and his black-rimmed glasses. He crossed his arms and frowned as I climbed the porch stairs.

"Why didn't you answer your phone, Cricket?" he asked, a stormy look crossing his handsome features. Uh oh, I had forgotten to call him back.

I sat my bag on the glider as I approached. "Well, I went to Grandma's apartment, and Gus told me she was gone. So,

I've been looking for her. I'm sorry... is she in here?" I pointed to his side of the duplex.

He nodded. "Yeah, she said she's moving back in."

"What?"

I moved past him and into the half of the duplex that Zeb rented from Grandma. There she was, making herself at home in what used to be her house before she had moved in with Gus. To be fair, the place looked almost exactly like the one I'd left Gus in a few hours ago. She walked around with a laundry basket, gathering up Zeb's dirty clothes that were strewn around the room.

"Grandma, what are you doing?" I took the basket from her.

She scoffed. "I'm cleaning up this pigsty, Cricket. What does it look like I'm doing? Why do you let him live like this?" she asked, whispering that last line while glaring at Zeb, who stood in the doorway, hands shoved into his pockets while he watched us.

"I don't let him—you know what, nevermind. Why are you here? Gus said you left the apartment days ago. Where have you been?" I asked, keeping a tight hold on the laundry basket while she tried to take it back from me.

She stopped and put her hands on her hips. "If you would ever answer when I call you, maybe you'd know why I left and what's going on. Did you think of that, missy?" she asked, glaring at me from behind her large, rose gold frames.

I huffed. Her feelings were clearly hurt. Yes, I'd been selfishly avoiding her calls and texts lately, and now I felt guilty. "I'm sorry, Grandma. I've had a lot on my mind lately." I sat the laundry basket on the floor and guided her to sit on the couch with me. "What happened?" I asked softly, putting one arm around her. I glanced at Zeb, who motioned to me that he was going over to my side of the duplex, and I nodded at him.

She laid her head on my shoulder, frowning. "Oh, Cricket, it's just awful."

"What did he do?" I asked, gearing myself up to head back to Forever Young to give that old man a piece of my mind.

She raised her head up to look at me and took my hand, squeezing it. "I think Gus..." Her eyes brimmed with tears.

"What?"

"It's just so terrible. I can't say it." She looked away, wiping the tears from underneath her glasses.

I sighed, biting the inside of my lip to keep from snapping at her. "Well, you're gonna have to, Grandma. What did he do?"

She leaned closer to me as if someone might overhear her when we were all alone. "I think he's a drug dealer, Cricket!" she whispered, then slapped a hand over her mouth, eyes wide.

I closed my eyes briefly and rubbed my forehead, trying to keep from losing it. "What makes you think that, Grandma?"

She threw her hands up and looked at me with dewy eyes as if it should be obvious. "The late-night phone calls, his office that I'm not allowed to go into, people showing up at all hours to pick up 'packages.' What else could he be doing?"

I paused, trying to think of a logical explanation to offer her, and came up blank. I couldn't very well tell her that Gus was a powerful warlock and although semi-retired, he still dabbled in spells and curses. Not knowing what else to say, I simply said, "He's not a drug dealer."

"Cricket, you don't know anything about the seedy

underworld of drugs and crime. I watched 'Breaking Bad.' I can recognize the signs, and they're all there. My fiance is a drug lord!" She clutched my hand.

Oh boy. "Grandma…" I started, shaking my head, not knowing how to convince her that her eighty-three-year-old fiance was not a drug lord without bursting into laughter at the thought.

"The other night, a man came by the apartment at midnight! Midnight, can you believe it? Anyway, he told me he was there to discuss purchasing a 'custom bag' from Gus," she said, scoffing. "What does that even mean? Who talks about a 'custom bag' in the middle of the night? Nobody, that's who," she went on, but I was barely listening.

I rubbed my temples. It was going to be hard to convince Grandma otherwise, now that she'd decided this man coming by in the middle of the night was hard evidence of Gus being a drug dealer.

"Are you listening to me?" she asked, her eyes still damp and a frown still firmly on her lips.

"Yeah, Grandma," I blinked a few times and tried to concentrate.

"Well, as soon as that strange man left, I told Gus I couldn't take it anymore. I packed a bag and stayed with Lynette next door for a couple of nights. She helped me realize I can't go back to such a toxic environment," Grandma said, her face distressed.

I sighed. "Look, maybe it's nothing. Or maybe he's planning a surprise for you?" I was grasping at straws.

"Oh, Cricket," she said, placing her hand on my cheek. "I know, it's hard to accept. The families of criminals are the ones who suffer the most," she added, nodding.

"But—"

"I'm going to a support group meeting tomorrow for

people who have family members involved in drugs. Will you go with me?" she implored, still gripping my hand tightly.

I waved my other hand vaguely in the general direction of Zeb and my side of the duplex, "Oh, I don't know, Zeb and I—"

She interrupted me again. "Zeb will understand. That one's a keeper, Cricket." She narrowed her eyes and patted my hand. Then she stood up, lifting her glasses so she could wipe away the last of her tears.

"Now, we have to get Zeb's stuff moved over to your place so I can get moved back in! It's going to be so much fun living next door to my girls again!" she exclaimed, wrapping me up in a suffocating hug.

8

———

"Just the girl I've been looking for. Sit," I said, using my "mom means business" voice when Mac came down the stairs with a scowl already on her face. Apparently, it was time to have a heart-to-heart chat with my teenage daughter.

"What?" she asked in that whiny, incredulous teenage tone I'd heard way too often lately. She flopped down on the couch opposite me, slouched down in the cushions, and crossed her arms. Her pretty face contorted into a grimace while she shot daggers at me with her eyes.

"When I got home yesterday, your car wasn't here, and neither were you. Did you forget you were grounded?" I put the book I'd been reading aside before picking up my coffee mug and taking a sip while I waited for her explanation.

She scoffed and rolled her eyes. "Seriously? I needed a new mascara, so I went to get one. What's the big deal?"

I raised my eyebrows at her. "The 'big deal' is that you were grounded from your car all weekend because you broke the rules Friday night. I don't care what you needed. You were grounded." She shook her head and turned away from me, but I continued, "And now you're grounded until next weekend."

She snapped her head toward me, eyes blazing with anger. "You have no right to ground me from MY car. Grandma bought it for ME."

"Yes, yes she did. And you are MY daughter. And what's yours is mine until you're eighteen, so I say you're grounded from our car until further notice." I took a sip of my coffee, trying to keep my cool.

"This is so unfair! I'm calling Grandma," she said, reaching for her phone and punching the screen so hard with her finger, I feared she would break it.

I smiled sweetly. "No need. She moved back into her old place yesterday, which you would have known if you'd been here. So, go next door and tell her all about it, if you want. Drop your keys on the counter on your way out," I added, watching her stomp to the front door. She tossed her car keys on the counter, as requested, before slamming the door behind her.

Teenagers—such a blessing. I finished my coffee and thought back to the talk I'd had with Regina about Mac and how Mac had seemed so much moodier and angstier than usual lately. Did it have anything to do with the ring, as Regina had suggested? I was contemplating that when my phone rang. "I'm a Werewolf, Baby" by The Tragically Hip meant it was Joey, and a grin tugged at my lips as I answered.

"Hey, Joe, what's up?" I asked, my smile evident in the tone of my voice.

"Oh, you know. Wolf stuff," he said with a laugh. His deep, southern voice echoing through the phone made my heart do flip-flops. Ho Cricket bit her lip while Logical Cricket smacked the back of her head.

I laughed a lot harder than his statement called for.

"Sounds exciting. It's not the same around here without you, you know…"

He sighed. "Yeah, I know." After a beat, he added, "I miss you, Cricket."

Sparks ricocheted inside my chest. I leaned back into the couch cushions, phone cradled to my ear. "I miss you, too."

He was silent for a moment, then groaned. "How are things with the Reaper?"

I chuckled. "Zeb and I are good, actually. But a lot is going on here. I wish we could talk about it over a beer at The Nail."

"Well," he said, drawing the word out and sounding like he was settling in for a long chat, "we can talk about it now. Go grab a beer and tell me what's up."

I shook my head, smiling even though he couldn't see me. "It's too early for beer, and it's too much to get into over the phone. Plus, you have enough to worry about as interim Alpha right now." I fiddled with the hem of my shirt. "How's the search going for a replacement, by the way?" I hoped they'd found someone so he could come back home soon.

"There are a couple of promising candidates, but nothing has been decided yet. Don't try to change the subject, babe. What's going on?" he asked, not letting it go.

I rolled my eyes. "Fine. Long story short, we have a dragon shifter in our midst, and it's my job to figure out what he's doing here, which hasn't been easy. He started dating Essie, too. And Grandma is convinced that Gus is a drug dealer, so she moved back into her old place. Oh, she bought Mac a car without asking me, too." I paused. "You're probably glad you're in Kentucky after hearing all of that," I added with a laugh.

Joey's deep laugh resonated through the phone. "Wow,

never a dull moment around you, babe. So, if Grandma is moving back in, where's Zeb gonna be living?"

"That's the part you're focusing on, Joe?" I asked as he laughed. "Did you not hear the part about the dragon?"

"Yeah, sorry. I know the answer to that question anyway, so don't say it," he said jokingly, although I knew he wasn't really joking.

We still had feelings for each other. There was no denying it. No matter how hard we tried to go back to being "just friends," I wasn't sure those feelings would ever go away. And I wasn't sure what that meant for Zeb and me. I loved Zeb. But I was coming to realize I loved Joey, too.

"Just be careful with the dragon, Cricket," Joey continued. "Since I can't be there, I'm glad Zeb is there for you. Make sure you keep him in the loop about your research, okay?"

I didn't want to tell Joey that Zeb was determined to give Aiden a chance, for Essie's sake, so I just said, "I will. Don't worry about me."

"I always worry about you, Cricket," he said, his voice deep with unspoken emotion. "Listen, I've gotta run, but please keep me posted. And stay safe for me, got it?"

"Got it. Talk to you soon," I said softly, hanging up and holding the phone to my chest, confusion and guilt swirling in my head. How could I feel so strongly about both of them? I didn't know what the solution was, but at least I didn't have to figure it out today.

LATER THAT EVENING, Grandma knocked on my door wearing her purple tracksuit that spelled "juicy" across her butt, with her white, crocheted bag hanging on her arm. Her hair framed her face in perfect silver curls, and though she smiled, there was sadness in her eyes. She missed Gus.

"Is that what you're wearing to TITS, Cricket?" she asked without saying hello. I rolled my eyes. "TITS" stood for "Together Individuals Tackle Sobriety," which was the support group Grandma had signed us up for. Because of Gus's alleged drug dealing. I was tempted to smack my own forehead, but I refrained.

I looked down at my outfit, a vintage Led Zeppelin T-shirt, jeans, and a mustard-colored cardigan. I also wore my favorite tall boots, and a pair of sunglasses were perched on my head as I grabbed my crossbody bag and travel mug of coffee.

"Why, what's wrong with it?" I asked, looking at Zeb, who sat on the couch, silently asking him to confirm that my outfit was fine.

"You look swell, Princess," Zeb said with a smirk, laughing when I flipped him a bird.

"I just think you could put a little more effort into your appearance, Cricket," Grandma said, shaking her head as she appraised my outfit once again.

"I think I'll start taking fashion advice from a woman who has 'juicy' scrawled across her ass when pigs fly, okay? Let's go," I said while Zeb struggled to keep his composure on the couch.

"You don't want to be late for TITS," Zeb said, almost doubling over with laughter.

Grandma shrugged and waved goodbye to Zeb as we headed out.

GRANDMA and I arrived at a church in downtown Nashville. We made our way inside, shaking hands and smiling at everyone, then stopping to pour ourselves some coffee before taking a seat.

"Do you really think this is necessary?" I asked, looking around the room. There were people from all walks of life here, in various stages of recovery, and I didn't feel like I could relate to any of them. Gus was not a drug dealer. We had no real reason to be here, for God's sake. It felt weird, almost like we were making a mockery out of other people's genuine pain and suffering, but Grandma didn't know the truth, and there was no way I could tell her.

Grandma huffed, placing her crocheted handbag on her lap. "We can't help Gus, so we have to help ourselves. We have to do this for us, Cricket."

I bit my tongue, wanting to tell her so badly. But maybe she was right; although we weren't actually victims of drug abuse, maybe we could learn something tonight. I decided to make the most of the situation and turned my attention to the woman at the podium starting the meeting.

"Cricket? Oh my God!" I heard a familiar voice hiss and turned to see Essie sliding into the empty seat beside me. She grabbed my arm and pulled me in for a cheek kiss, beaming at me. She gave Grandma a little wave and then whispered, "What are you two doing here?"

I rolled my eyes and nodded toward Grandma. "It's a long story. I'll tell you later." She glanced at Grandma and raised an eyebrow. Then we listened as people took turns going up front, introducing themselves and sharing their struggles.

I paid close attention to the speakers, becoming caught up in their stories, feeling their pain. It was eye-opening, and I thanked God that we didn't actually have a drug dealer in the family. I only wished I knew how to convince Grandma of that.

When it was over, people began mingling, hugging one another, sitting together with cups of coffee, even crying together. I felt we had overstayed our welcome at that point and wanted to drag Grandma out of there before some well-meaning soul came over to chat, and Grandma started spilling the beans about her drug-dealing fiancé. Before I could steer Grandma out of the conference room, Essie picked up our previous conversation.

"So, what brings you two to TITS?"

I closed my eyes for a second and willed myself not to laugh.

"Oh, Essie. We've just found out the worst news about Gus," Grandma said, reaching for Essie's hand. "He's been dealing drugs, right under my nose! Can you believe it?" She patted her nose with a Kleenex.

Essie looked at me, mouth hanging open.

I shrugged and shook my head. "Yeah, we're all broken up about it. Grandma, can you grab me a fresh coffee?" I asked, trying to get rid of her so I could fill Essie in, then get us out of here.

"Of course, sweetie." Grandma tottered toward the coffee maker, and I turned back to Essie with a sigh.

"She thinks Gus is a drug dealer because people have been coming over at all hours of the night. I couldn't think of any other excuse, so here we are... at TITS." I covered my mouth to stifle a laugh while Essie didn't bother.

She barked a laugh, then clamped her mouth shut when a woman sitting on a nearby couch scowled at us. "Oh, that's rich. As you Tennesseans say, 'Bless her heart.'" Essie chuckled, watching Grandma, who was engaged in conversation by the cookies.

"Yeah, so what are you doing here?" I asked.

"I've been coming to TITS for years. I've never mentioned it, but I had a bit of a drug and alcohol problem in my earlier years."

"I had no idea. Wow," I said, meaning it. There was much I didn't know about Essie, apparently.

"Plus, Aiden and I had a fight, so I wanted to get out of the house for a bit." She grimaced, taking a sip of her coffee.

Now we were getting somewhere, and I didn't even have to bring him up. "Oh? What's going on?" I tried not to act too interested and failed.

Essie smiled. "I know you don't like him, Cricket. But he's a good guy. He's just under a lot of stress from his family lately. And this relic he's supposed to find, he's out of his mind with worry about it."

"I'm sure he is. Do you know what it is he's looking for exactly?" I asked. *Smooth*, Logical Cricket piped up, rolling her eyes. I elbowed her in the ribs.

"I'm not really supposed to—" Her hand was at her neck, reaching for something that wasn't there. Her eyes went wide. "Oh, no."

"What's wrong?"

She looked down, still feeling her chest and neck with one hand. She looked back at me, eyes full of fear. She whispered, "My firestone. It's gone!"

BACK AT THE DUPLEX, Zeb rubbed the stubble on his jaw as he listened to Essie describe where she last saw her firestone for the third time. He paced the living room while Essie and I sat on the couch, me trying to comfort her by rubbing her arm.

"I don't understand. I had it this morning. I put it back on after my shower. Where could it be?" Essie's eyes brimmed with tears.

"Alright, we need to recreate your day. We'll go everywhere you went and look for it." Zeb reached for his jacket, which was lying on the couch.

"Or... we ask Aiden where it is," I said. They both turned incredulous stares on me.

"Cricket!" Essie exclaimed. Zeb threw his jacket back on the couch and glared at me, his hands on his hips.

"I'm just saying. It's not out of the realm of possibility that he could have taken it." I shrugged. The fact that I had two Grim Reapers scowling in my direction didn't deter me. "It can't hurt to ask him about it."

"Why would you automatically assume Aiden stole it?" Zeb asked, a stormy look on his face.

"He was in her house! He's been with her night and day. Why would you automatically assume he didn't?" I retorted. He threw his hands up in the air.

"Look, I know your firestone is connected to you, it's your ticket through the veil, and it holds a certain amount of power over you. Wouldn't a Reaper's firestone qualify as a valuable artifact? An 'antique' or 'relic,' if you will?" I asked, leading them with my line of questioning.

Essie scoffed. "Aiden would never do that to me, Cricket. You don't know him like I do."

"And you've only known him for a few weeks, Essie. I hate to be the bearer of bad news, but he could've been pulling the wool over your eyes all this time." I shrugged, avoiding meeting Zeb's stony stare.

"If she says he didn't do it, he didn't do it." Zeb turned away from me, picked up his jacket again, and motioned for Essie to follow him. "We're going to retrace your steps today, see if we can figure out where you might have lost it."

Essie scowled at me, then stood to join Zeb. I glanced between the two of them, who were already heading toward the front door.

"Wait, I'll come, too."

Zeb stopped me with one hand raised. "It would probably be better if you didn't, Cricket."

I felt as if he had plunged an icy sword through my heart. The look he gave me was cold, and a chill ran down my spine. "Oh."

Essie gave me a little shrug, then followed Zeb out the door. I stood there for a few moments after I heard them pull out of the driveway, then I grabbed my crossbody bag off the counter.

If they wouldn't confront Aiden about it, I would.

9

I stood in front of Essie's apartment inside a luxury high-rise building in downtown Nashville. I'd only been here once before, but I remembered the apartment was a posh three-bedroom on the fifteenth floor with a hell of a view. I knocked, hoping Aiden was here so I could talk to him alone. Zeb and Essie were out searching God only knew where for her firestone when I was convinced it was right here under our noses—with Aiden.

After the third knock, I started wondering if a credit card would really open a locked door like in the movies, when Aiden finally opened the door a crack. Without a word, he went to slam it in my face, but I stuck my foot in the jamb just in time.

"Open up, Aiden. I have a bone to pick with you." I glared at him, my lips pressed in a straight line. Reluctantly, he opened the door wide enough to allow me in.

"Say what you have to say, then get out." He reached for a tumbler of whiskey, which sat on the coffee table. Essie's place looked like a spread out of Luxury Home Magazine with its ten-foot ceiling, shiny hardwood floor, and private balcony access from the living room. A large, leather sofa and matching recliner filled the living area while the adjoining kitchen sparkled with stainless steel appliances and marble countertops. I drew my attention back to Aiden, who had sat down on the sofa with his drink, looking at me expectantly with a scowl on his face.

I took a deep breath, deciding not to beat around the bush. "Why did you take Essie's firestone?" I crossed my arms and popped one hip out, hoping I projected more confidence than I felt.

He chuckled silently for a moment, lowering his eyes to the drink in his hand. "I don't have her firestone," he said in a dark, raspy voice, void of all emotion. He met my gaze and his fierce expression put my Revealer senses into overdrive. I not only felt his aura, I saw waves rolling off of him, causing the air to shimmer with heat. The faint metallic tang that alerted me to his dragon form the first time we met lingered in the air. He sat there, holding his tumbler of whiskey with one hand, stroking the rim with his thumb, looking as if he wanted to burn me to ashes where I stood.

"I don't believe you." I swallowed the fear that rose in my chest as he stared at me. My stomach turned as the scent of metal and ash grew stronger.

"I really don't care what you believe, Cricket. You should go."

Not knowing what else I could do, I turned to leave, figuring I'd call Zeb and make him tell me where he and Essie were so I could join them, whether Zeb liked it or not. With my hand on the doorknob, I sent one last glare Aiden's way when I heard a noise coming from the back of the apartment.

I looked at Aiden, whose eyes went wide. Forgetting about leaving, I strode in the direction of the noise, which sounded like a deep, rumbling roar. Shivers coursed down my spine, but I shook them off as I went in search of whatever was making the horrible sound.

"Cricket, get out of here." Aiden was on my heels as I roamed through the apartment, ignoring him and peeking into each room, the growling sound getting louder with each step I took.

I reached the last room in the hallway. This had to be it. The door was already ajar. I nudged the door open further and looked inside. What I saw stopped me in my tracks.

"No!" I heard Aiden's deep voice echo in my ear before my vision went dark.

I HEARD VOICES, muffled and garbled. My head throbbed with a dull ache, and my mouth felt like I'd been sucking on cotton balls. I opened my eyes to the harsh, bright fluorescent lighting in the unfamiliar room. I was lying in a bed, and Zeb stood nearby, talking to a man in a white coat. I looked at my arms; needles and tubes led to machines that buzzed and beeped.

"Wha..." I tried to ask what was happening, where I was, but only the one syllable came out. It was enough to attract the attention of Zeb and the other man, who I had to assume was a doctor.

"Cricket! Thank God," Zeb said, relief in his voice. He took my hand in his, squeezing it as he leaned down to plant a kiss on my forehead.

"Careful, she still needs her rest," the doctor said, placing his hand on my wrist. My pulse must have been satisfactory. He nodded to Zeb, smiled at me, then left us alone.

"What happened?" I asked. My tongue felt two sizes too big for my mouth as I spoke, the words feeling foreign as they came out.

Zeb sat on the edge of my bed, stroking the back of my hand and smiling at me. "They say you passed out. Took quite a knock to the head when you fell." His eyes glimmered as if he were holding back tears. "You gave us quite a scare, Princess." He raised my hand to his lips, brushing a kiss against my knuckles.

"Passed out?" I asked, rubbing my eyes with the hand Zeb wasn't holding. I didn't remember passing out. But would one remember that? I wasn't sure. The last thing I remembered was being at Essie's apartment—with Aiden.

"Yeah, you had a tumble when you fainted. I'm just glad you weren't alone when it happened. Aiden brought you to the hospital and called me straight away. He said you'd come over to help look for Essie's firestone." Zeb pushed my hair back behind my ear as he spoke, his voice gentle and soothing.

I wrinkled my nose, my brows drawing together in confusion. "Aiden? I don't remember passing out. Something else was going on…" Then a thought occurred to me.

"How long have I been here?"

Zeb grimaced. "Three days, Princess. You've been in and out of consciousness, and the doctor wanted to watch you for bleeding or swelling in your brain. He said you could suffer from some memory loss, too." He stroked my hair, still sitting beside me on the bed.

I sat up, feeling a sudden urgency to get up to speed on things. "Where's Mac? And Grandma? Did you call Carl? Where's my phone?" I fired questions at Zeb, one after another, not giving him time to respond. He held his hands up, a grin tugging at the corners of his mouth.

"Slow down, Cricket." He laughed, pulling my phone from his jacket pocket and handing it to me. As he did, his thumb brushed the home button, which lit up the screen. I glimpsed some missed texts, and my eye caught on Joey's name. I'd have to call him later, too.

"I called Carl. He said to take it easy for now and to call him when you're up to it. He sent flowers, too." Zeb nodded toward the huge basket of lilies next to the television. "Mac and Grandma are fine. They've been spending a lot of time here but went home a couple of hours ago. They'll be glad to see you awake when they return tomorrow." He smiled down at me, then sighed.

"You scared the shit out of me, Cricket. I don't know what I'd do without you." His eyes grew damp with tears, and I noticed how tired he looked, the bags under his eyes, and his disheveled hair.

I mustered up a little grin and patted his hand. "I'm sorry, Zeb. I don't know what happened." I squeezed my eyes shut for a moment and shook my head. "It feels like something is missing. Something else happened, but I can't remember what it was."

"Don't worry about it now. It'll come to you." He smiled warmly at me and brushed a kiss against my cheek. The door to my room opened, and a nurse poked her head inside.

"Visiting hours are over, sir." She gave Zeb a pointed look, then retreated, letting the door close behind her.

"I'll come back early tomorrow, Princess. Maybe they'll let me take you home." He grinned, rising from my bed to stand. With one last kiss to the top of my head, he picked up his coat from the foot of my bed.

"Oh, wait. Did Essie find her firestone?" I asked.

He stopped as he reached the door and turned to me,

face crestfallen. "No, not yet. See you tomorrow, Princess."
Then he was gone.

———

"CRICKET, WHY AREN'T YOU EATING?" Grandma Betty asked.
She scowled as she looked at the untouched plate of lasagna
in front of me. I had picked at my salad and taken a few bites
of garlic bread, but I didn't have much of an appetite.

Since leaving the hospital two days ago, I felt out of
sorts. Per doctor's orders, I had done little except lay on the
couch, watch HGTV, and try not to let Grandma smother
me with comfort food. She barely left my side, and though I
knew she meant well, it was becoming annoying.

"I'm not really hungry, Grandma." I pushed a cherry
tomato around on my plate for a show of good faith, then
gave up and laid my fork down.

She pursed her lips and raised an eyebrow at me. "You've
got to eat something, hungry or not. Can I make you a sandwich?" she asked, rising to head back into the kitchen.

I rolled my eyes. "Sit. I don't want anything. I'll eat when
I'm hungry, okay?"

She huffed. "Suit yourself. I don't know why I bother to
cook for you girls. You won't eat anything I make you."

She glanced at Mac, who smirked. "Maybe if anyone in
this house besides me cared about the ethical treatment of
animals, I could eat something other than salad." She
stuffed a forkful of lettuce into her mouth to prove her
point.

Grandma shook her head. "At least Zeb appreciates a
good home-cooked meal. When will he be home?"
Grandma started clearing the table, removing my plate with
one last glare at me.

"I'm not sure. He's been hanging out with Aiden a lot lately." Which didn't please me at all. I may not have remembered exactly what happened the night I allegedly passed out, but I remembered everything before that. I was willing to bet money Aiden hadn't saved me from splitting my head open. If anything, he was responsible for putting me in the hospital. But I had no proof.

Grandma beamed. "Oh, that Aiden, he sure is something, isn't he?"

"He's something, alright," I agreed through gritted teeth.

"I'm so grateful he was there when you fainted! Things could've been so much worse!" She retreated to the kitchen, hands full of dirty dishes. I turned to Mac, who was still diligently working on her salad.

"Haven't seen much of you lately. What's going on?" I placed my napkin on the table and took a sip of sweet tea.

Mac shrugged. As usual, she was dressed in mostly black, makeup was on point, and her long black-dyed hair hung loose over one shoulder. "Nothing much. Just hanging out."

I squinted at her. I remembered everything Regina had told me about how weird Mac had been acting lately and how she'd even broken up with Luther. But I couldn't say anything about it. Otherwise, she'd know Regina had told me, and I didn't want Regina to regret coming to me.

"How's Luther? You should invite him over for dinner sometime. I promise I'll cook something vegan."

Mac shifted in her chair and didn't meet my gaze. "Oh, I don't know. He's been really busy helping his dad at the garage."

I smiled brightly. "Nonsense. Invite him over one night this week, I insist."

She bit her lip and cut her eyes at me. "Whatever. I have

to go." She stood, grabbed her black backpack off the hook by the back door and pulled her keys out of the front pocket.

"Where are you off to?" I asked, glancing at the clock, which was not lost on her. She scowled.

"I'll be back before dark, Mom."

Before I could say anything else, she was out the back door. She obviously didn't want to tell me she had broken up with Luther, and I wondered why. She was also being very secretive about where she was going, which would generally worry me. But since my last conversation with Regina, I had ordered a remote tracking device, which now sat in the bottom of Mac's backpack. She had no idea it was there, and maybe it was shady on my part, but at least I didn't have to worry about where she was.

I pulled up the tracking app and watched as Mac's car headed down our road, away from Bitter End, while I finished my sweet tea. I heard the front door open and looked up to see Zeb walking into the dining room—with Aiden in tow.

Zeb grinned and came over to plant a kiss on my cheek. "Princess, did you save us some dinner?"

I glared at him, then glared at Aiden. "We saved *you* some dinner, guess you'll have to share it with the stray you brought home."

Zeb frowned while Aiden laughed. "Someone is feeling better, I see. I'm glad, Cricket. You gave us all quite the scare." Aiden stood there, hands stuffed into the pockets of his skinny jeans.

Ho Cricket, the skeptic, piped up. *"He doesn't mean any of that. Why can't you remember what happened, Cricket?"*

Logical Cricket spoke up as well. *"I can't believe I'm saying this, but she's right. This guy can't be trusted."* For once, I didn't have to shove them into a closet in the back of my mind because we were all in agreement. Something was up with Aiden Rhys, and it seemed I was the only one who could see it.

Zeb smiled at Aiden and clapped him on the shoulder. "That she did, mate. And we have you to thank for being there to help. God knows what could've happened otherwise."

Grandma popped back into the dining room, two ice-cold beers in her hands. "I thought I heard you boys come in!" She passed the beers to Zeb and Aiden while I looked at her in annoyance.

"Cricket, you shouldn't be drinking beer right now, not after what you've been through. Would you like some more sweet tea?" she asked me while smiling sweetly at Aiden and patting her perfect silver curls.

"No thanks, I'm good." Grandma ignored me and circled around the table to Aiden, clasping his hand that wasn't holding the beer.

"Aiden, thank you so much for being there for Cricket. You don't know what it means to me." Aiden blushed and glanced at me with the briefest hint of a smirk.

"We're very grateful, indeed. Aren't we, Cricket?" Zeb asked. Everyone turned to me.

"You know, I'm exhausted. I think I'll turn in early." I stood and patted Zeb on the shoulder as I made my way past him and Aiden.

"What? It's still early." Zeb checked his watch and shot me an incredulous glance.

I heaved a sigh. "I'm tired, okay?" I turned to go when a brief flash of me, winding my way through a hallway, burst into my head, along with a roaring sound. I reached out to steady myself on the doorframe, but almost as quickly as it had come, the image was gone again.

"Alright, Cricket?" Zeb asked, reaching for me.

I regained my composure and shook my head. "Yeah, I just need to lie down. See you in the morning, okay?" I asked Zeb, who put his arms around me and gave me a soft kiss before letting me go.

"Sleep well," Aiden said just as I exited the dining room. I resisted the urge to flip him a bird, deciding it wasn't worth the effort.

I made my way up the stairs to my bed, wondering what the hell that image was about. The hallway and the awful noise I'd heard in my head for only a couple of seconds. Was it a memory of that night? If so, how could I recover the rest of it?

I WAS DRIFTING off to sleep, the sounds of Zeb and Aiden's laughter from downstairs finally dying down, when my phone vibrated on the nightstand. I cracked one eye open and saw Joey's name. I figured I'd better answer. I only sent him one brief text to let him know I was okay after getting out of the hospital. He was probably worried. Not to mention, I missed him, too.

Babe, how RU? I need an update.

I'm fine, sorry to worry you. So much has happened! I wish you were here.

Wish granted :) Be home in a couple of days, can't stay long tho. I wanna CU.

My breath caught in my throat. Joey was coming home!

But only for a few days, I reminded myself quickly. That was better than nothing, though.

> You just made my night, can't wait!

I can think of better ways to make ur nite lol

I sent an eye-rolling emoji since that's what I was actually doing while reading that last message.

> I'll bet lol

I'd rather do that in person tho. Sweet dreams.

That message was followed by a smiley devil emoji from Joey. A smile tugged at my lips as I yawned and put the phone back on my nightstand.

Sweet dreams, indeed.

It was late as I walked into The Rusty Nail, the crisp night air making goosebumps appear on my skin. Johnny Cash's "Ring of Fire" played loudly on the jukebox, but the place was empty. Except for Joey, who stood behind the bar wearing a tuxedo with his white towel draped over one shoulder while he poured a shot of vodka, then slid it across the bar to me. I took a barstool. I wore a long, sequined gold dress with a slit up to my hip and a neckline down to my navel.

"Joey? What's going on?" I asked. I didn't understand why we were all dressed up at The Nail, and no one else was here. Johnny Cash continued to croon about falling down,

down, down into the ring of fire while Joey nodded at the drink he poured for me.

"Bottoms up, babe." His lips turned up in a sexy half-smile as he took me in, eyes dark and blazing as he came around to my side of the bar. I downed the shot, alcohol burning its way down my throat as he approached me.

Joey pulled me to my feet, then turned me around so my back was to him. He raised my arm, putting it behind his neck, then let his finger sensually trace its way back down. Past my elbow, then my armpit, which elicited a giggle from me, a la Baby in "Dirty Dancing" when she and Johnny practiced their dance moves. He spun me around, and suddenly we were slow dancing; the music had abruptly changed to "Feel It" by Michele Morrone from the "365 Days" movie I just watched on Netflix a few nights ago.

Joey wound my hair around his fist, pulling me back to whisper in my ear. "Admit it, Cricket. This is what you want, what you've always wanted." His breath was hot against my skin as he spoke. He nipped at my earlobe while he released my hair. His hands roamed up the front of my scantily cut dress, finding the deep cut neckline and tracing it with his fingers, making me shiver. He cupped my breasts and kissed his way from my earlobe, down my neck, to my shoulder.

"What do you mean, Joey?" I asked, gasping as his touch set me on fire. I looked around to find the bar full of people now. When had that happened? An older woman with gray hair scowled at me, shaking her head as she watched what Joey did to me. I recoiled from him, placing my arms across my chest. I turned to face him and found him staring at me, eyes full of adoration and one hand stretched out toward me.

"You know what I mean, Cricket. We're meant to be together." Static electricity from his wolf crackled in the air as he gazed at me, waiting for me to take his hand. I glanced around the bar again—so many people, it was so loud. With an apologetic glance at Joey, I dashed through the bar toward the restrooms, passing the disapproving woman on my way, who was still frowning at me.

I found the bathroom and was relieved that it was a single-occupancy unit: one toilet and one sink. I closed the door behind me and turned on the faucet, splashing cold water on my face. Soon the doorknob turned, and Joey was inside the bathroom with me. He locked the door behind him, spun me around, and before I knew what was happening, he had me pinned to the wall, kissing me, over and over. His tongue found mine as his hands moved up and down my body.

"Joey," I moaned against his lips as we kissed. "Is this a dream?"

He caught my lower lip in his and sucked it gently, growling as he did. "I don't know, babe, but if it is, I don't ever want to wake up." His mouth moved from mine, kissing down my neck, then he nipped at my ear, whispering, "You drive me wild, Cricket."

I smiled against his mouth as he kissed me again, my hands pushing his tuxedo jacket off his shoulders. He pushed the straps of my gown down my arms, exposing my bare skin to him. He kissed my neck, my collarbone, and the slope of my breasts. I unzipped his pants and slid my hand inside to feel his length, hard and ready. I wrapped my hand around him and stroked as he teased my nipple with his tongue.

He moaned, and I spun us around until he was leaning against the sink. I began lowering myself down, down, farther down until my lips were on the head of his cock. I looked up, locking eyes with him, and licked my lips. He smiled and put one hand in my hair, the other he used to brace himself against the sink.

I let my tongue trace him while I wrapped my hand around the base. He whispered, "Cricket," and closed his eyes. I ran my tongue down the length of him, teasing and tormenting. He threw his head back, his hand combing through my hair. He shuddered as I worked him, my head bobbing up and down as he groaned my name, over and over.

Finally, he pulled me up by my elbows to face him and kissed me hard. Then he turned me around so I was facing the mirror, my hands gripping the sides of the sink. He locked eyes with my reflection and leaned up until his lips grazed my ear. I could feel him rock hard against my ass. I arched back into him, meeting his eyes in the mirror. He gave me that smoldering smile and kissed my earlobe, then my neck.

"You're all mine," he said with a soft smile and planted a kiss on my bare shoulder. He whipped the skirt of my gown aside, the deep slit making it easy to push aside. I felt his hard length against my bare ass, and I moaned.

"Joey," I said, my voice low and raspy. I was ready for him. I needed him now.

One hand caressed my ass while the other gripped my hip. I watched him in the mirror as he admired my backside. I bit my lip and caught his eye in the reflection. The corner of his mouth turned up in a half-smile as both hands gripped my hips, and he thrust into me, hard and deep.

Slowly at first, he thrust again and again. I moved to meet him, matching his strokes as they became faster and faster. I gasped. "Joey..." I said as he watched me in the mirror, his eyes dark and full of desire.

He smirked and smacked my ass, thrusting harder and

faster until we were both panting and gasping. Finally, he yelled, "Cricket!" We came together, and he collapsed against my back as I sagged against the sink with satisfaction and exhaustion.

He kissed my shoulder and caressed my arms, still lying against me. "You're incredible," he said, panting.

I jolted upright in bed when my alarm sounded, heart racing. I looked down at myself, still in my pajamas. "Holy hell," I whispered, flopping back down onto the bed. I picked my phone up off the nightstand to shut off the alarm, then noticed the time. Nine A.M. I was supposed to meet Gus for lunch in a few hours to discuss a plan for getting Grandma to move back in with him. I scowled. I decided the first order of today's business should be a long, cold shower as the memory of that dream came rushing back to me, heat flushing my cheeks.

"Stupid alarm."

10

"Cricket! Thanks for meeting me," Gus said, sitting down in the booth across from me. He shot me a somber half-smile and clasped his hands together on the tabletop. He wore his usual uniform, which consisted of dark sunglasses, fedora hat, and khaki Members Only jacket. He had called me and asked to meet to discuss the "Grandma thinks Gus is a drug dealer" situation, so I agreed to meet him at a diner in East Nashville for lunch.

Gus was in his eighties and was a highly respected and powerful warlock. Grandma had moved in with him at Forever Young after only knowing him for about two weeks, and I objected at first but had come to realize that he wasn't so bad once you got to know him. He helped me get a handle on my Revealer abilities and had chosen not to throw me under the bus several times when Carl questioned my training progress. For that, I would remain eternally grateful and in his debt.

"No worries. I actually need to talk to you about some things too, but first—what are we gonna do about Grandma?" I took a sip from the Diet Coke our waitress had just placed in front of me.

He threw his hands in the air. "The woman is exasperating. A drug dealer?"

I stifled a giggle.

"It's your own fault for letting people pick up curses and potions at your apartment all hours of the night. What should I try to convince her you're doing instead? I can't go to another TITS meeting, Gus."

He chuckled. "Don't worry. I'll come up with something. You just have to convince her to meet with me." His expression turned serious, then he said, "I miss her like crazy, you know."

I reached across the table and squeezed his hand. "I know. And she misses you, too. She's just insane."

He barked a laugh. "You got that right. So, do you think you could convince her to have dinner with me soon?"

"Leave it to me, Gus. She'll be there if I have to drag her kicking and screaming. Now, next order of business—Aiden Rhys," I said as the waitress came by for our orders. After she left, I could feel Gus's eyes narrowing at me from behind his sunglasses.

"The dragon shifter? What about him?"

I took a deep breath. Where to start? "Well, remember how I told you about meeting him initially? How I realized what he was?" Gus nodded and motioned for me to go on. "It's like my Revealer senses have taken on a mind of their own—they don't like Aiden. I have intense feelings of mistrust and dislike when I'm around him."

Gus's bushy eyebrows rose above his dark glasses. "That's interesting. You know, I've heard of abilities like yours... 'evolving' over time. Let me see what I can find out about it in some books I have at home."

"That's not all, though. Mac is acting strange, Essie is behaving like a smitten teenager over Aiden, and her fire-stone has gone missing. Zeb is telling me there's nothing to worry about. And apparently, I 'fainted' in Aiden's presence recently, and now everyone is praising him for saving me from splitting my head open. And I have no memory of what actually happened, although I'd be willing to bet money that it didn't go down like that." I crossed my arms and sat back in the booth, waiting for Gus to process that information and give me his take on the situation.

"One of the first things I ever learned in my magical training was this—don't trust a dragon. They're only out for themselves. They'll stop at nothing to get what they want. Especially when it comes to money and power." He stabbed the air with his index finger to drive the point home.

Our food arrived then, and I stuck a French fry in my mouth as I contemplated Gus's words. "Speaking of money and power, he's supposedly in town because he's trying to locate some antique or relic that a client of his wants to buy. Aiden's family owns an antique shop in Atlanta, and he said he'd received a tip that the item was here, but he wouldn't say what it is. Any ideas?"

Gus scoffed. "I'd say there's more to that story. My guess is the 'client' is non-existent; whatever he's searching for, it's for his own personal gain. And whatever the item is, it's either worth a lot of money, or it holds a great deal of power."

"Do you know about any kind of supernatural relics that could be stashed somewhere in Nashville, maybe something that he could sell for a small fortune or that would grant him some sort of mystical capability?" I asked between bites of my hamburger.

Gus ate in silence for a few moments. "You mentioned Essie's firestone went missing?" he asked, tentatively.

I threw my head back. "Thank you. Yes! I told Zeb and Essie that Aiden probably stole her firestone, and they wouldn't hear of it. That has to be it, right?"

Gus shrugged. "Owning a Reaper's firestone is like owning a piece of their soul. Whoever possesses it could potentially compel the Reaper to do anything they wanted. And you know one thing Reapers do best? Send people to Hell." Gus bit into his burger while I bit down on the fingernail of my thumb.

"So, you're saying that theoretically, if Aiden has the stone, he could have Essie kill people for him?" That was bad news. The worst news.

"That's what I'm saying."

"I guess that would be a neat trick to have up your sleeve, but I feel like something is missing. Like maybe the firestone and Essie are a means to an end. But I'm having trouble putting all the puzzle pieces together." I scowled at the remains of my burger. I pushed the plate back and bit down on my lips, thinking.

"You could be on to something. My advice? Keep an eye on Essie. If he really has her firestone, it won't be long before he uses it." Gus nodded at me, and I felt my blood run cold as I finished my fries.

I thought about what he had said as Gus and I said our goodbyes at the end of our meal. I needed to see Essie again and soon.

"I PROMISE, I'll be super careful." Mac and Regina stood in the living room, both with their hands clasped in front of them as if in prayer. I put my book down and glanced toward the window; it was already dusk.

"You know the rules. No driving after dark."

She rolled her moss green eyes at me. "Seriously? Mom, I'm like the only sixteen-year-old who has to be home by 5pm. Come on, please?"

"Where did you want to go? Maybe I can drive you," I offered, which prompted horrified glances between the two girls.

"We uhh... were going to work on a school project at Luther's house. I know the way there like the back of my hand, Mom. Why can't I drive?" she asked, giving Regina a quick look. Regina met my gaze briefly.

I decided to play along. "Why don't you have Luther come over here? I miss seeing that boy anyway. I'll make veggie burgers for dinner, and y'all can have the living room to work on the project." I picked my book up as if the matter was settled and tried to stifle a giggle after seeing the look on her face.

"You're being ridiculous. All of our... supplies are already at Luther's house. Right, Regina?" she asked, turning to her friend for confirmation. Regina cast her eyes downward as she nodded in agreement.

"Sorry, Mac. Rules are rules. I don't make them. Oh wait, yes, I do." I flipped my book open to the wrinkled Walgreen's receipt that held my place and pretended to read.

Mac heaved a sigh and threw her hands up in the air. "Why are you like this?"

I glanced up from my book with a raised eyebrow. "What do you mean? A delight to be around? I can't help it. It just comes naturally."

She stuck her tongue out at me and stomped into the

kitchen with Regina in her wake. Regina threw back an apologetic glance at me and I grinned.

I went back to my book and tried to figure out where I'd left off when there was a knock at the front door. I sighed, setting my book on the coffee table with a wistful glance, and rose to see who had the audacity to come over unannounced.

"Cricket! I hope I'm not interrupting anything?" Essie asked, standing on my front porch holding a bottle of wine. Her black-streaked platinum blonde hair glowed in the moonlight, and her emerald eyes sparkled as she smiled, holding the bottle up for my inspection. "Thought we could have a girl's night in, just the two of us!"

Who was I to turn down free alcohol on a Wednesday night? "Come on in," I said with a laugh, holding the door open wide enough for her to slide past me.

"Although, it won't be just the two of us. Mac and Regina are in the kitchen pouting because I won't let them take the car out after dark." I took the bottle from her, which was still cold.

"Oh yeah? Well, maybe they'd like to join us." At my raised eyebrow, she continued, "Well, not for the wine, obvs!"

I laughed, taking a couple of wine glasses and a bottle opener from the cabinet in the adjoining dining room. I brought them over to the couch with me, where Essie had already made herself at home.

"If you're up for some teenage angst and drama. Because that's on the agenda for tonight, it would seem." I poured a glass for each of us and settled back into the couch cushions to relax when Mac busted into the living room again, Regina following close behind. She stopped mid-stride, the frown on her face dissolving into a barely visible smile.

"Oh, hey, Essie. What are you doing here?" she asked, trying to feign disinterest, but I knew better. Mac loved Essie since they shared the same love of black clothing, dark makeup, and the goth aesthetic in general. Back when Essie had stayed with us while I recovered from the beatings I'd received when I was kidnapped by Joey's brother, she'd had the time of her life staying up late, sharing makeup tips and music recommendations with the gorgeous Australian. Something told me her tune about needing to take the car out tonight was about to change.

Essie directed a stunning smile towards Mac and Regina. "Mac, Regina! Cricket just told me you girls were in for the night. How lucky!" Essie patted the space on the couch next to her in an invitation to sit.

"Lucky, indeed," I muttered as the girls sat down.

"So, tell me what the two of you have been up to lately?" Essie asked, prompting a thousand-watt smile to appear on Mac's face. Maybe the angsty portion of the evening was over now.

"The usual stuff. I added a ton of new makeup vids to my TikTok. Oh, and Regina and I have been finding some really cool vintage clothing and jewelry at the thrift shops." She stopped and pointed to the faded Ramones T-shirt she wore. "Like this. It's an authentic tour T-shirt from the 80s! Oh, and this," she said, holding out her right hand, where the large emerald costume jewelry ring was perched.

Essie reached for her hand, examining the bright green ring. "This is gorg! I love it! Where on earth did you find it?" she asked, turning Mac's hand one way, then the other, getting a closer look at the ring.

"A little shop on Clinton. We actually found a trunk full of cool stuff there!" Mac beamed while Regina smiled softly, looking between Essie and Mac. I sat back, sipping my wine, watching the exchange.

"It's absolutely stunning. I'm jelly," Essie said, winking at Mac as she let go of her hand.

Mac giggled. Yes, giggled. "Thanks! You should go with us sometime."

"I'll take you up on that offer when we have enough daylight left to take the car out for a spin." Essie grinned at me, and I rolled my eyes.

Mac glared in my direction briefly, then turned a bright smile in Essie's direction. "Deal!"

"Hey, I offered to drive you two over to Luther's house, you know," I said, frowning as I downed the last of my wine.

Mac rolled her eyes in dismissal, then continued her conversation with Essie while I shared a meaningful glance with Regina. Something wasn't right here, and I was going to find out what it was.

11

"God, I've missed you!" I exclaimed, hugging Joey tightly. His arms wrapped around my waist, pulling me close. It felt good to be in his arms again, too good. I backed away and adjusted my shirt, my face flushing with heat. I cut my eyes to Joey, and a lopsided grin was plastered on his face.

"I'm glad to hear it. I thought maybe you'd forgotten all about me." He winked and gestured to the booth for me to sit. Joey had texted me earlier in the day to say he was back in town, and we'd made plans to meet at The Rusty Nail.

I wrinkled my nose and tilted my head to the side. "Wait, what's your name again?"

"For the record, I've missed you too, Cricket." His dark eyes met mine, filled with desire. I looked away and bit my lip. We were supposed to go back to being just friends, but that was obviously going to be hard to do. I still felt the attraction, and I know Joey did too. I could see it in the way he looked at me.

I cleared my throat after the waitress brought our beers.

I immediately took a swig of mine and said, "So, tell me all the New Haven gossip."

Joey barked a laugh. "We got a new gas station on Highway 11. That about covers it. I think you should fill me in on what's been happening here." He took a drink from his beer and waited for me to start.

I let out a heavy sigh. "I don't even know where to start, Joe. I think it all has to do with Aiden, the dragon shifter, but I don't have any proof. I can't even remember what happened the night I fainted at Essie's apartment, and he supposedly rescued me." Joey scowled, but I continued before he could say anything, "It's almost as if my Revealer senses are trying to warn me about something, but I can't figure out what it is."

"Hmm. What's Zeb's take on it?" he asked, rubbing his chin.

I rolled my eyes. "Zeb thinks I'm overreacting. He's too busy thanking Aiden for taking me to the hospital when I passed out to worry about anything else. In fact, he asked me to take it easy on Aiden since he's making Essie so happy." I shook my head.

Joey blinked in surprise. "That's not at all what I was expecting." His brows knit together in worry as he reached across the table to squeeze my hand. "What's *your* take on the situation? What do you really think is going on?"

The question took me aback. I'd been so focused on what Zeb thought, what Essie thought, what everyone else thought about Aiden that I hadn't stopped to gather my own thoughts, aside from the initial distrust I felt toward him. "Well, I think whatever Aiden is looking for is dangerous, and it would benefit his family." I stopped, remembering some of my interactions with Aiden. "I think he's using Essie." That had been in the back of my mind, but I hadn't put it into words before. It felt good to get it out. I looked up to see Joey smiling at me.

"I think you should go with your instincts, babe. Don't let anyone, including Zeb, talk you out of it."

"Thanks. I know you're right. And I will." I paused, eyes still locked on him. The corner of Joey's mouth quirked up into a half-smile, and he ran one hand through his unruly curls.

"Cricket..." he said, drawing my name out in that deep southern accent of his. "What are we doing?"

"What do you mean?" But I knew exactly what he meant. I took him in, his dark, messy hair, his russet brown eyes, and the way they looked at me with longing. His muscles rippled beneath the tight black T-shirt he wore. All I had to do was say the word, and Joey would be mine. I knew that, and it was so tempting. We were so good together, and I wondered if it had anything to do with Joey imprinting on me. But there was Zeb. I loved him too, even though things were strained with him right now.

He smirked at me. "This. Right here. Fighting it." He finished his beer, then looked away from me. "Nevermind. I know the answer."

Zeb.

"Joey..." I didn't know what to say. I loved them both.

He took my hand again, his thumb tracing circles on the back of it. "Take a good hard look at your relationship with Zeb, okay? Ask yourself if it's what you want. And don't worry about how he's going to feel or how I'm going to feel. I think Zeb and I have one thing in common at least—we both want you to be happy."

I sucked my lower lip between my teeth and nodded without looking at him. "I will. Joey, I—"

"And stop apologizing. I knew what I was getting into

when I gave you my heart, Cricket." A hint of a smile crept onto his face, and my heart squeezed. What was I doing? Joey supported me, encouraged me, loved me. And I had rejected him. Had I made the wrong choice?

I couldn't sit here any longer with him. I had to think. I needed to talk to Zeb. And I still needed to figure Aiden out. I grabbed my bag, made my apologies to Joey, promising to call him, then headed out.

12

————

On my way home, Zeb texted me to say he had a job and wouldn't be home when I got there. That meant he had to go be a Reaper, so someone had died, or someone was about to die who wasn't supposed to yet. That's what his job entailed. My plan to talk to him about our relationship was foiled, so I decided I needed to do something. I had too much energy. My brain was whirling with information and emotions. I kept circling back to what Joey said, that I should trust my instincts about Aiden and go with my gut. I needed to see Aiden. Not only because of my suspicions about him, but also because I wanted to know what exactly happened when I passed out. I took the nearest exit and headed back downtown to Essie's apartment.

I stood in front of Essie's door once again, feeling a sense of deja vu. Maybe being here would help me remember. I knocked. After a few moments, I was about to turn and leave when I heard a noise inside, then the door opened.

"Cricket. What are you doing here again?" Aiden asked, his eyes stormy. He glanced behind him, then back to me.

"Hello to you too. Could I have a word?" I all but barged into the place, pushing past him. I stopped in my tracks before I made it to the couch; something seemed off. I spun to look at Aiden, who seemed the same. But my senses picked up... more. I wasn't sure what it was. It was just *more*.

I narrowed my eyes and put my hands on my hips. "What's going on? Where's Essie?"

He rolled his eyes. "She's working tonight with Zeb. I'll ask again. What are you doing here?"

"I'm gonna be straight with you, Aiden. I think you're up to no good. I think you took Essie's firestone, and I think you're using it to make her... I don't know, do something." I waved my hands in the air. "Maybe I don't know everything yet, but I know one thing—you're trouble. And I'm gonna find out what's going on."

As I spoke, I circled the room, picking up books and trinkets, looking them over and replacing them. I stepped into the kitchen with Aiden on my heels.

"What the fuck do you think you're doing?" He grabbed my arm. I jerked loose from him and continued my search. For what, I wasn't sure, but I figured there had to be something incriminating around here.

"Essie is my friend, and she's in trouble. Let go of me!" I yelled when he grabbed for me again. I dodged him, made it back to the door, and headed into the living room before he could try again. Looking behind me, I collided with a solid object in my path. With an "oomph," I righted myself and turned to see an actual dragon in Essie's living room.

Sitting in the middle of the large room, its tail curled around its legs, sat an enormous dragon with a murderous expression on its face. Mossy green and gold scales covered it, seeming iridescent in the apartment's bright lighting. Its chest heaved as it breathed deeply, tendrils of smoke and small wisps of flame visible with each exhale. It spread its huge, translucent wings as it glared at me as if to invoke fear in my heart. Mission accomplished. A breath hitched in my throat as I attempted a scream, but nothing came out.

Aiden sauntered out of the kitchen then, a smile erupting on his pompous face as he took in the scene. "Dad, meet Cricket. Cricket, Dad." He crossed his arms and leaned against a bookcase, looking between the two of us.

"This is your dad?" I asked, finally able to produce sounds.

The dragon snarled, and with a final huff, emitting a wisp of smoke and flickering sparks, he began to change. I watched in amazement as the wings retreated into the dragon's back. The scales receded, revealing human skin beneath. Bones and cartilage cracked and snapped as the dragon reconstructed itself into a new form. The tail disappeared, and the gigantic creature shrunk in size until only an elderly human man remained in its place. Entirely naked, I might add.

I averted my gaze while Aiden smirked. He reached for a blanket on the back of a nearby chair and tossed it at his dad. I allowed enough time for him to cover himself with it, then faced Aiden's father.

"Cricket, I've heard so much about you." Aiden's father managed to look intimidating, even with only a quilt wrapped around his waist. He was tall, slim, his graying hair was slicked back. His grey eyes stared at me coldly as he stood there, jaw clenched as he ridiculously clutched the blanket around himself. "Pity we haven't met until now. Weren't you in the hospital recently?"

A chill ran down my spine at his words. He said it almost as if insinuating he had something to do with it. Did he have something to do with it? I couldn't remember.

"I was. How do you know about that?" I asked.

Aidan stepped between us, holding one hand up. "Now, Dad, no need to bring up that awful night. I'm sure Cricket doesn't want to remember it—it could've ended so much worse for her." The aura I always sensed around Aiden grew stronger, the metallic tang hanging in the air and feeling sharp in my lungs. I thought I caught a tendril of smoke as it disappeared behind him. His eyes flashed brightly as he glanced at me, as if in warning.

"Does Essie know he's here?"

Aiden scoffed. "Essie knows, and she's fine with it. She's fine with most everything these days."

"Forgive my son for his ill-manners. I'm Stephan Rhys, Elder of the Atlanta Clutch. You just saw me in my draconian form. I do apologize. We weren't expecting company," he said in his thick southern drawl. I wanted to tell him to go put some clothes on, but something told me that the blanket still draped precariously around his hips was for my benefit only. He seemed like he wouldn't mind being naked in a room full of people—if they were uncomfortable with it, that was their problem, not his.

I didn't know what was going on here, but my Revealer senses were pinging like crazy, telling me to get the hell out of there. I backed toward the door, not wanting to turn my back on them. "I need to find Essie," I said. My hand reached behind me for the doorknob.

Stephen stepped toward me. "So soon? We were just getting to know one another. You see, my son is not nearly as competent as I gave him credit for." He glared at Aiden, who looked chagrined. "I could use your help."

I laughed. "You think I would help you? I don't know what you're looking for, but I'd be willing to bet it's not for a client—it's for you. And if you want it so badly, that means whatever it is, it can't be good news for the rest of us.

"Don't make me do this the hard way, Cricket." Stephan's hard eyes appraised me, narrowing as he made what sounded like a threat to me.

Finally, my hand made contact with the doorknob. I flung it open without another word to either of them, heart racing. Not only did I just see a dragon sitting in Essie's living room, but I was also pretty sure Stephan had low-key threatened my life in there. I needed to find Zeb and Essie, and fast.

I ARRIVED at the duplex to find Essie and Zeb there, having completed their work for the night. They were laughing and having beers in the living room when I walked in and placed my bag on the kitchen counter. After Grandma had moved back in, the porch felt like it wasn't ours anymore, so we'd stopped hanging out there.

"Did you see the look on his face, Sebby?" Essie asked, both of them laughing.

"Hey guys," I said, interrupting. "We need to talk."

Zeb looked up, the laughter dissolving from his expression. "What's going on, Cricket?" It wasn't lost on me that he hadn't called me Princess much lately. I decided to think more about that later, though.

"Essie, I just came from your apartment. Did you know Aiden's dad was there?" I asked, crossing my arms.

She frowned. "Yes, he's staying for a few days. Why do you ask?"

"He all but threatened me. Also, Aiden basically

admitted to having your firestone." Zeb and Essie exchanged looks before looking at me.

"Cricket..." Essie began, shaking her head.

"What? You don't believe me?" I asked incredulously.

"Where is this coming from? Aiden brought you to the hospital when you passed out, probably saved you from injuring yourself badly. And you're accusing him of stealing and his dad of threatening you? Seriously?" Zeb threw his hands up.

I turned narrowed eyes on him. "Are you seriously questioning me on this? Ever since Aiden got here, you've been on his side at every turn. I don't get it. Why don't you guys just exchange friendship bracelets since you're BFFs now?" He huffed, smirking at me. I turned to Essie. "You, I can understand. He has your firestone, so you're under his influence."

"You're wrong. I'm not under a spell or anything like that. Aiden has been nothing but good to me. And to you, for that matter," Essie added, looking at me with teary eyes.

I looked from one to the other of them, both of them glaring at me disapprovingly. "Fine. I'll do this on my own." I marched to the counter and grabbed my crossbody bag, looping it over my head while the two of them watched me. Zeb, with anger in his eyes and Essie, with sorrow. "Thanks for nothing." I slammed the door behind me as I headed to my car.

———

I DIDN'T REALLY KNOW what to do next. I just knew I had to get away from those two, so I drove to the nearest Sonic for a milkshake and decided to just keep on driving. I was so angry that they didn't believe me, especially Zeb. Essie was being brainwashed, so she had an excuse, but he didn't. He was actively choosing to believe Aiden over me. That hurt, bad.

I was driving down backroads, slurping a strawberry milkshake with Led Zeppelin blasting, when my phone rang. I knew from the ring tone; it was Joey, so I answered it through BlueTooth in the car.

"Babe, what's up? You ran out on me so fast. I was worried about you."

I grimaced. "Sorry, Joe. I just—I needed to talk to Zeb. But that was a mistake."

"What happened?"

"You told me to trust my instincts, so I did. I went to Essie's apartment to confront Aiden—"

"Cricket…" Joey drawled.

"—and not only did he basically admit to stealing Essie's firestone, but his father was there in dragon form, and after he changed back, he threatened me." I was so frustrated. It all came out in an onslaught of word vomit.

"Wait, he threatened you?"

"At least you believe me! Zeb doesn't. In fact, he's angry with me because I'm not showing enough gratitude to Aiden for helping me." I let out a little scream and pounded on the steering wheel.

"Okay, first of all, you shouldn't have gone over there by yourself, Cricket. Second, what the hell is Zeb's problem?" Joey asked, sounding irritated.

"I don't know. But I'm tired of it." I sighed heavily, turning the car onto a side street.

After a few beats of silence, Joey spoke, "Look, I don't want to tell you what to do, but maybe you need to sit down with Zeb—without Essie—and talk things through."

He was right. We'd barely had a minute alone lately, it seemed. We needed to talk, just the two of us.

I pouted. "I know. You're right. I'm just... I'm just really disappointed in him right now." I pulled the car into a well-lit lot in front of Wal-Mart and put it in park. I rested my forehead on the steering wheel.

"All the more reason you need to talk, babe."

I raised my head up and scowled. "Why are you pushing so hard for me to make up with Zeb?"

Joey laughed. "Look, if anyone wants to see you break up with him, it's me. But I want you to be happy, and for a long time, it seemed like Zeb was what made you happiest. I don't want you to throw that away if you can get it back."

"Joey..." I said, dragging the word out into about four syllables.

"Thank me later. I've gotta run."

I said goodbye to Joey and drove around a bit more before going back to the duplex. I knew Joey was right, but I wasn't in the mood to deal with Zeb right now. I figured we would just end up fighting some more. So I knocked on Grandma's door instead, hoping she was still awake.

After a moment, I heard her shuffling around inside, and the door opened. She was in a floral nightgown, her hair was in curlers. "Cricket! What are you doing here so late?" she asked, patting her hair and peering behind me.

"Can I come in?"

She raised an eyebrow and opened her mouth to speak, but I cut her off.

"Please, just don't ask. I don't feel like talking about it right now. Can I just come in?"

Her expression softened, and she opened the door up wider. "Of course you can."

I entered the side of the duplex that Zeb had previously

rented from Grandma. It had only been a couple of weeks, and the place still felt like him, even smelled like him. Grandma Betty took my elbow and turned me to face her, then opened her arms up to me. I walked right into them, letting her embrace me without a word. I let the tears of frustration, confusion, and anger come flooding out as she held me, patting my back and rocking us slightly.

THE NEXT MORNING I sat in Grandma's living room with a cup of coffee, waiting for Zeb to leave. Although I was furious with him, I trusted him and knew Mac was safe with a Reaper watching over her. It was early and I couldn't sleep, so I figured I might as well get up and make some coffee. Soon, Grandma came tottering into the room, her curlers disheveled.

"It's awfully early, Cricket." She yawned and came to join me on the couch.

"Sorry if I woke you. I made coffee, want some?"

"In a bit. Thanks," she said. Then after a moment, she added, "Wanna talk about it?"

I nodded my head yes and said, "No."

She laughed. "I'm gonna take a stab at it and guess something's happened between you and Zeb." She paused, glancing at me for confirmation. I shrugged and gave a small nod. "Well then, do you think hiding over here is going to help matters?" she asked, reaching out to rub my arm.

"I'm not hiding. I just needed to breathe for a minute." I smiled at her, then remembered why she was here. I narrowed my eyes at her. "You're one to talk. Aren't you doing the same thing? Hiding here in the duplex instead of talking things out with Gus?"

She frowned and swatted at my arm. "Oh, Cricket. It's not the same thing. Is Zeb selling drugs?"

"No, and neither is Gus."

"All the evidence points to it." She crossed her arms, looking ridiculous in her gown and curlers while trying to argue with me.

"Evidence shmevidence. You need to talk to him. I'll bet there's a reasonable explanation that doesn't involve OxyContins," I said, giving her shoulder a little nudge with my own.

She sighed and rolled her eyes. "I do miss him. And that thing he does—"

"STOP." I put my hands over my ears and she laughed.

We sat silently for a few minutes, watching the living room grow lighter, the smell of coffee thick in the air. "If I talk to Zeb, will you talk to Gus?" I asked, breaking the silence.

"I suppose I could."

I grinned as I raised my mug to my lips.

13

I walked into my side of the duplex and tossed my bag on the counter. Zeb was in front of the television, eating cereal on the couch, while Mac sat in the recliner with a cup of coffee. Zeb gave me a curious look but continued eating his cereal.

"Where were you?" Mac asked, scowling at me. "You left me here with him." She nodded at Zeb, who smirked in response.

"I was at Grandma's." I glanced at Zeb for a reaction.

"Why?" he asked, not even looking at me.

I rolled my eyes and didn't answer him; I just flopped down on the couch.

Mac looked between the two of us over her coffee mug. "Okay, this tension is too much. I'm out of here." She flipped her black hair over her shoulder and took her coffee up the stairs to her bedroom, slamming the door behind her.

I shuffled myself around to face Zeb. "We need to talk, don't you think?"

He sighed and glanced at me, sitting his empty bowl on the coffee table. "I don't really know what more to say,

Cricket. We've talked about this several times already. You keep agreeing to lay off of Aiden, but it doesn't last." He shrugged.

I glared at him. "Why are you so 'Team Aiden'? You barely know the guy. How can you be so sure my suspicions are unfounded?"

"You don't understand. Essie's been through a lot. She lost the only man she ever loved years ago. It was traumatic for her, and she's never been truly happy since. Until now." I saw a glimmer of tears appear in his eyes as he spoke.

I sighed. "I get that, I do. And it's sweet that you care so much about your friend's happiness, but Zeb." I stopped, gesturing between the two of us. "We are a couple. If you're mad at someone, I'm mad at them, too. If I suspect a lone dragon shifter in our midst, you should too." I sat back and crossed my arms, tears pricking my eyes. "It hurts that you don't believe me."

His lips turned down in a frown, and he ran one hand through his hair. "It's not that I don't believe you. I believe that you believe something is going on with Aiden. I just don't understand because from where I sit, the bloke seems like proper gold."

I nodded, biting the inside of my lip and trying to hold back the tears. "So, you won't even try to see it from my perspective?"

"I'll try. Alright?"

I nodded, not really believing he would try, but hoping he would. He held out his arms to me, and I stood, going to him and letting him embrace me. It felt warm in his arms, but an underlying coldness was there, waiting to break through the surface. I felt the tension between us; the thick, icy wall that was there now, with Aiden Rhys perched at the top of it.

STILL FEELING like a storm cloud hovered over my head regarding the Zeb situation, I managed to pull myself together the next day in the hopes of getting Grandma and Gus to make up.

"Cricket, I just don't know about this." Grandma fussed with her perfect silver curls, then smoothed the wrinkles out of her yellow skirt as we waited at a local coffee shop for Gus. I rolled my eyes. I had gotten them both to agree to meet here to discuss Grandma's suspicions about Gus's work, and I'd be damned if they left here unreconciled. I could not go to another TITS meeting with her. I just couldn't.

"Relax, it'll be fine. Gus has a perfectly reasonable explanation for all of this, and then the two of you can go on with your lives. Together. At Forever Young." I sipped a latte and kept one eye on the door, hoping Gus would arrive soon with said reasonable explanation on the tip of his tongue.

Grandma tutted, then pursed her lips in a thin line. "I don't know of any other explanation there could be."

"Just hear him out, okay?"

The door chime sounded, and in walked Gus, looking the same as always in his uniform of sunglasses, fedora hat, and khaki Members Only jacket. He glanced around before spotting us, then started making his way over.

"There he is!" Grandma Betty gasped. I smiled. This would be easy for Gus, as long as he'd cooked up a good story.

He stopped in front of our table, making a little bow. "Hello, Betty. Cricket. Mind if I join you ladies?" he asked, his gaze lingering on Grandma. It was sickeningly sweet how much they seemed to miss each other, I had to admit.

Grandma made an attempt at indifference, but I saw right through her. My lips twitched from trying not to smile when she said, "I suppose," barely glancing his way.

I reached for my bag on the back of my seat. "I should probably let the two of you talk this out." I went to stand up, but Grandma placed a hand on my arm.

"Please stay, Cricket. I think you should hear this, too."

Should I, though? I sighed and sat back down, then gestured for Gus to have a seat with us. He obliged, sitting across from Grandma. He took a deep breath and glanced at me quickly. I nodded in encouragement.

"Betty, I miss you, and I want you to come home. I know you have questions about my line of work and its secretiveness, and I promise I can explain it all. There's nothing illegal going on, I promise you that." He reached across the table and took her hands in his. She allowed him to, although she continued to look away from him.

"I just don't know, Gus. You'll need to tell me everything about this job of yours and let me think about it."

Gus nodded. "That's fair. You see, I..." he trailed off, glancing at me. I shrugged and raised an eyebrow. Grandma cocked her head, waiting to hear his explanation.

"You... what?" she asked.

Gus scratched his forehead, raising his fedora hat up a bit as he did. "Well, I—I make puzzles." I gave him a "wtf" look while Grandma scowled.

"Puzzles?" Grandma asked ironically with a puzzled expression on her face.

"Yeah. Puzzles. Custom puzzles." He crossed his arms and leaned back in his chair, pleased with his explanation. I shook my head and closed my eyes momentarily as I sipped my latte.

"Gus, I'm not quite sure I understand." Grandma narrowed her eyes at him.

"Yeah, why don't you explain it to us?" I asked, then clamped my mouth shut to prevent a smile from erupting on my face.

He scowled at me. At least I thought he was scowling behind those dark glasses of his. "Well. I take custom orders online. Then I make their puzzle for them. It's pretty easy," Gus said, squirming in his chair. Poor guy, he thought Grandma would buy a simple explanation, but I knew better.

"But why do people come over in the middle of the night to pick up puzzles?"

I felt like I was watching a tennis match, my gaze bouncing from one to the other of them. So far, fifteen to love, in favor of Grandma.

Gus cleared his throat. "These puzzles... they're fragile. I can't mail them. They'd break." A sheen of sweat broke out on Gus's forehead.

"But at midnight?"

I stifled a laugh and bit my lip as Gus scrambled for another answer. "Yeah, most of my clients are busy. They work during the day. It's a service I provide, being open late."

Grandma frowned. "Can I see one of these puzzles? And why couldn't you have just told me about them in the first place?"

Gus laughed nervously. "Oh, I was a little embarrassed about it," he said, with a chuckle, then continued, "Sure, you can see one, but I don't have any right now. My latest client picked up last night. But I'll show you the next one."

Grandma's face lit up with an idea. "Maybe you can make a puzzle for me!"

My lips twitched with the effort it took not to giggle. I turned expectantly to Gus. Thirty to love, still Grandma.

"Oh, you don't even like puzzles," he said, waving dismissively.

"I would love a puzzle that you made especially for me!" Grandma exclaimed. She beamed at him while he removed a handkerchief from his pocket and dabbed at his face.

"Really? Well, they take a long time to make. It might be a while."

Grandma reached for Gus's hand. "That's okay. I'm willing to wait for it. I just know it'll be wonderful!"

"Yeah... wonderful," Gus agreed, looking at me with his eyebrows hovering above his sunglasses.

"So, Grandma. You're okay with Gus making custom puzzles and the late-night pickups?" I asked, trying to confirm she'd bought this half-cocked story hook, line, and sinker.

Grandma pursed her lips in thought for a moment before replying. "Well, it's not ideal, but you've got to admit, it's better than being a drug dealer!" She lowered her voice to a whisper on the last two words and leaned in closer to us.

"You've got a point there, Grandma," I agreed, biting back a laugh.

Grandma gasped, putting one hand to her mouth. "Cricket! That means we can't go to TITS anymore!"

"Oh no," I feigned disappointment as Gus's shoulders shook with laughter.

"TITS? This I've gotta hear about."

"I'll let Grandma fill you in on that. Are we good here? You're moving back to Forever Young?" I asked, clasping my hands together, eager to put this chapter of our lives behind us.

Grandma beamed, glancing first at me, then at Gus. "Yes!" she exclaimed, nodding her head in agreement. Gus took her hand in his and brought it to his lips, brushing a kiss against her knuckles. Her face went rosy as she grinned.

"I've missed you, Betty," he whispered. I felt Gus deserved a few points after she bought that ridiculous story and decided to call it a deuce.

MONDAY NIGHT I finally resumed my duties for the MVA, finishing a leave of absence due to my hospital stay and subsequent memory loss. I'd just left a meeting with Carl at Sunshine Cleaners and was about to pull out of the parking lot when my phone rang. "Don't Fear the Reaper" by Blue Oyster Cult filled the car, instantly telling me it was Zeb.

I answered on BlueTooth while turning onto the highway. "What's up?"

"Cricket! Have you talked to Essie today, by any chance?" Zeb asked, sounding frantic.

"No, not for a couple of days, actually. Why?"

He sighed heavily. "I needed her help on a job a bit ago. There was a fire at a club downtown, lots of people whose time wasn't up yet. Anyway, she never answered her phone and never showed up. I'm at her apartment now, and no one's home."

"Aiden's not there either? Or his dad?" I asked, pulling the car onto the interstate.

"No one. I was hoping she was with you, or you'd at least heard from her recently."

"Well, let's not panic yet. Maybe she and Aiden are out on a date, and she left her phone at home?"

"No, even without her phone, she'd have received the

message." I frowned at that, not understanding what he meant, but assumed he was talking about some sort of Reaper thing.

"Okay, then what should we do? Where should we look?" I was already taking the next exit to head back into town toward Essie's building.

"Go by The Rusty Nail and see if she's there by any chance. I know a few other places I can check in the meantime."

"Consider it done," I said, stepping on the gas.

"Thanks, Cricket. You're the best."

Feeling slightly annoyed but unsure why, I continued toward The Rusty Nail, hoping to find Essie and Aidan at the bar enjoying a beer together. The way there was like second nature, so I let my mind wander a bit as I drove.

It occurred to me that I didn't question Zeb's hunch that something was wrong. I just took him at his word and asked how I could help. *How very different from his reaction to my hunches about Aiden*, Logical Cricket said, poking her head out of the closet to remind me. I sighed. A conversation was in order with Zeb, but it would have to wait.

THE LAST THING I expected to see when I walked into The Rusty Nail was Joey behind the bar. There he was, a white towel thrown over his shoulder, mixing drinks and pouring beer. I stopped just as he looked up, surprise passing over his face, which quickly turned into a grin.

"Hey, babe!" he called to me. I sauntered over to the bar and took an empty stool right in front of him.

"What the hell are you doing back there? I thought you

were on leave or something," I said, glancing around the bar for any sign of Essie or Aiden.

Joey quirked a brow at me. "They were short-handed tonight, and I'm in town, so..." He poured a shot of vodka and passed it to me, but I pushed it back.

"I can't; I'm looking for Essie and Aiden. Have you seen either of them in here tonight?"

His brow furrowed as he thought for a bit. "No, don't think so. Why, what's going on?"

I groaned. "Zeb thinks Essie's in trouble. He hasn't heard from her all day, and he can't get ahold of her."

"And you're out looking for her?"

"Bingo," I said, picking up the shot glass of vodka I had previously refused and downed it.

Joey chuckled. "I get the feeling you're a little irritated." He leaned against the bar.

"He's so focused on Essie and Aiden lately. Can you blame me?" I rolled my eyes.

Joey shot me a cocky half-grin. "I don't blame you at all. Did you ever have that talk with Zeb?"

"I tried. It didn't go very well."

"Oh. Well, I'm sorry to hear that. Really." Joey put a hand over one of mine and squeezed. I gave him a look, and he laughed. "No, I really am. I just want you to be happy, Cricket."

I winced. "I'm sorry, Joey."

"Nothing to be sorry about. I just know what Zeb has, and he's taking it for granted." He stared at me with those dark eyes, full of desire.

Feeling bold, I bit my lip, then asked, "And what does he have?"

A smirk tugged at his mouth as he leaned closer to me. "He has what I want most."

He brushed the back of his hand against my cheek and under my chin, stroking my lower lip with his thumb. I tilted my eyes down, watching his hand and savoring his touch. It had been a while since Zeb had touched me like this or even spoken tender words to me. I leaned into Joey's touch, craving it.

Was it over with Zeb? I felt like it might be. Something had broken in our relationship. He seemed far away and out of my reach now. Should it always have been Joey? Had I only been prolonging the inevitable?

"I think I have to end it with Zeb."

Joey's hand stilled. "You're sure?"

I nodded, tears welling in my eyes.

He walked around to the other side of the bar and wrapped his arms around me while I let it sink in. I had to end things with Zeb. I loved him, but he had deserted me lately, leaving me feeling alone and frustrated. He made me feel like second place, and that wasn't fair to me. I didn't want to settle. I shouldn't have to settle. I deserved more.

I pulled back from his embrace, wiping my eyes. "Okay, I need to keep searching for Essie and then…"

Joey nodded solemnly. "Do what you need to do, babe. I'm here if you need me. Always."

14

I went home after searching some more bars downtown and driving around in Essie's neighborhood. It was late, and I hadn't seen either her or Aiden anywhere, but I dreaded going home and facing Zeb and what I needed to do. I pulled into the duplex and saw that Mac's car was gone. My temper flared. She knew she wasn't supposed to be out late, and it was way after dark now. I slammed the car door behind me as I stomped up the stairs and into the house, pulling my phone out of my bag to text her.

> Mac, where are you? It's late, come home. Now.

Several minutes went by while I sat on the couch, staring at my phone and waiting for the three little dots to appear to show she was replying. They never came. I tried again.

> I'm not joking. I need you to reply and let me know where you are and if you're okay.

Still, nothing. I walked through the house, inspecting each room for signs of her or her things. Her backpack was missing, as well as her coat. And Zeb wasn't here either, so I picked up my phone again to text him.

> Zeb, where are you? Mac's not home.

Soon, the three little dots appeared, then his reply.

> still looking for E. guessing you had no luck? I haven't heard from Mac.

> no luck.

I began making calls, starting with Regina. It went straight to her voicemail, so I left a brief message, then I tried Luther, not thinking about how late it was. I woke him up, and he groggily answered that he hadn't seen or heard from Mac in days. My stomach was in knots and felt like I swallowed a lead ball.

A sinking feeling came over me, and I tried to tell myself that Mac was fine. She was just being a rebellious teenager and staying out past curfew. I'd done it myself many times when I was younger, too. But I couldn't shake the feeling that something wasn't right.

Then I remembered the remote tracking device I had placed in Mac's backpack. I opened up the app on my phone and saw the tiny dot indicating Mac was in downtown Nashville. I zoomed in and saw it was a location on Clinton Street, and I remembered the antique shop.

What was she doing there in the middle of the night?

I picked up my bag and keys, texting Zeb on my way out the door. I was about to find out.

I stood in front of the antique shop on Clinton Street and peered inside the darkened windows. It didn't appear that anyone was inside, but the tracker on my phone said otherwise. I didn't see Mac's car, however, so I supposed it could be wrong. Maybe she dropped the tracker inside the store last time she was there? All I knew was that I had to find out if my daughter was in there and why. And if this was just a case of teenage rebellion, she was going to be grounded until kingdom come.

I took out my phone again and sent another text to Mac.

> Mac, answer me.

I heard the faint chime of a cell phone almost immediately after I hit send and whirled around. It sounded like it had come from inside the shop. I stepped up to the door and tried the knob, which was locked. I knocked on the door, but of course, no one answered.

It didn't make sense that both her tracker and her cell phone were in the shop, and she wasn't. I banged on the door again, harder this time. "Mac, are you in there?" I yelled, the knot in my stomach growing larger by the second.

"Cricket, what's going on?" Zeb said from behind me. I'd sent him a text when I left the house, asking him to meet me here, but I didn't say why.

I held up my phone with the tracker on the screen. "Mac wasn't home, and the tracker I put in her backpack shows that she's inside this shop." He quirked an eyebrow when I mentioned the tracker. "Don't judge me. Anyway, I just called her phone and heard it ringing from inside."

He frowned and tried the doorknob. As if I hadn't already. I rolled my eyes and held back a sigh. Then he peeked inside the windows, just like I had done. I bit the inside of my lip to keep from screaming.

"You're sure?" he asked.

I released a heavy sigh, not even trying to hold it back. "I'm sure. Open the damn door."

Zeb examined the hinges briefly and nodded. He stood back and gave the door a well-placed kick with his black combat boot, striking the lock. It shuddered but didn't budge, so he tried it again, kicking harder. This time, the door burst inward, opening the shop to us.

He tentatively stepped inside, holding up one hand to indicate that I should wait. I didn't. I was on his heels, heading inside the store with him. He threw me a scowl and continued through the shop. I didn't see anything except antiques and was starting to feel hopeless when I finally heard a shuffle coming from the back.

I charged ahead of Zeb while he harshly whispered, "Cricket!" I ignored him and kept moving, finally reaching what appeared to be a back bedroom of the old house that served as an antique shop. I flung the door open, ignoring Zeb's warnings from behind me.

Inside was the last thing I expected to see—Essie, standing over my daughter and Regina, who were both bound and gagged.

Stunned for a moment, Zeb spoke before I could. "What the bloody hell is this, Essie?" he asked, gesturing at the girls. He made a move toward them, then Essie stepped in his path.

"I can't let you do that, Zeb." She radiated crackling energy, the kind I associated with Zeb as a Reaper. The air pulsed around her, and she put her arm out to block Zeb when he tried again. There was a look in her eyes I hadn't seen before.

"Mmmph!" Mac said, and I rushed to her while Essie was distracted with Zeb. I tried to remove the gag from her mouth, but it was tied so tightly I couldn't get a good grip on it. Regina's eyes were wide, and when I followed her gaze, I saw Essie moving toward me. Her fist connected with my face so hard, I flew backward into a shelf of antique books, knocking most of them to the ground around me.

I rubbed my face, stunned that Essie had actually just hit me. Zeb was just as confused as I was, but he quickly assessed the situation and made a grab for Essie. Reaper against Reaper, they lunged, dodged, and struck each other over and over, and I couldn't tell who was winning. I stole glances at them while still trying to untie the bindings on Mac's wrists.

Again, I was interrupted by a kick to my side, skidding me across the floor into Regina. I groaned, clutching my side and wondering if I had internal bleeding. Damn, that hurt. Essie tossed a glare at me while blocking an uppercut from Zeb as I tried to stand.

"What the fuck?" I yelled at her as she came at me again after striking Zeb.

"I'm sorry I have to do this, Cricket." Her voice was strained as if she was channeling someone else. I immediately knew what was going on.

"Zeb!" I called out to him after she slammed me against the wall. "It's Aiden. He has her firestone. He's doing this!"

Confusion spread across his face, catching him off guard and allowing Essie to knock him on his ass. She reached into her coat pocket and produced a length of silver cord, which she slapped onto Zeb's wrists. He howled in pain, incapacitated and shaking on the floor.

"What did you do to him? I know it's you, Aiden." I stood as best I could, still holding my side. She approached, an ugly smirk on her beautiful face, twisting her black-painted lips into a snarl. She tossed her black-streaked platinum hair over her shoulder as she came to a stop in front of me. Mac and Regina squirmed in the background, trying to break free from their bindings, groaning and trying to scream with the gags stuffed into their mouths.

"Do I look like Aiden to you, bitch?" she asked, just before her fist met my face and everything went dark.

WHEN I REGAINED CONSCIOUSNESS, I found myself bound and sitting between Regina and Mac, with Zeb lying by the bookcase, books scattered all around us on the floor. The gags had been removed from the girls' mouths, and Essie hadn't bothered to gag Zeb or me. I guessed it was time to talk.

"Mom!" Mac exclaimed when she saw me stirring. She and Regina wore tight smiles and frequently glanced at the door as I held my head and blinked, trying to get my bearings. Zeb was out cold. He laid on the ground, unmoving, his eyes closed. At least I hoped he was out cold. I couldn't think about the alternative right now.

"What's going on, Mrs. Jones?" Regina asked, her brows furrowed and her lips down-turned.

I winced as pain sliced through my side and abdomen from Essie's repeated kicks to my gut. "That's an excellent question, Regina." One I only had partial answers for. "Do you know where she went?" I asked, taking in the small room and not seeing any signs of Essie.

Mac shook her head, "No, she didn't say. She only said she'd be back and not to try anything."

"Okay. Okay." I rubbed my temples, thinking. No doubt she'd gone to get Aiden, but why did she have the girls here? I felt like I was trying to get from point A to point D and had missed B and C somewhere along the way.

Zeb stirred, moaning and shifting on the floor a bit before falling silent again. I turned to the girls. I had to ask questions now. We didn't know when Essie would be back and what would happen next.

"How did she get you to come here? What has she told you?" I had to tread carefully here. To my knowledge, my teenage daughter still had no clue about the supernatural world, and I wanted to keep it that way if I could. She still thought Nina, my vampire boss who had kidnapped her a few months ago, had been driven insane with grief because her husband was dying, which led to her kidnapping Mac. And she thought that I had been the victim of a car-jacking gone wrong when Joey's Alpha wolf brother, Drake, had kidnapped and beaten me.

Mac glanced at Regina for confirmation as she told me the story. "Essie group texted us earlier and asked if we would mind showing her this antique shop, where we found the trunk full of costume jewelry and clothing. She said she'd already talked to you and that you said it would be okay for me to take the car out after dark." She looked sheepish as she said that last part, then added, "Sorry, Mom."

My heart squeezed. To think she was even worried about that right now. Silly girl. "It's fine, sweetie," I said, smiling at her. "What else did she say?"

"She wanted us to meet her at the Starbucks down the street, then we all walked here. I told her it looked like the place was closed, but she said she had called ahead and the owner had left us the key under the doormat," Regina said, then bit her lip. "I guess we were kind of dumb to believe that."

I sighed. They trusted Essie. It didn't surprise me they wouldn't have questioned anything she said. We'd had her stay in our home before. Why wouldn't they trust her? "Don't worry about that now. Anything else? She could be back any minute."

"Once she opened the door, she locked it behind us and said the owner told her she had a new shipment of vintage clothes in the back room that we could look through before she put them out on the floor tomorrow. So, we ran back here, and that's when she used that thing over there to knock Regina down first, then me," Mac said, nodding to a large antique vase sitting on the desk in the corner. Of course, she'd go for Regina first. Regina was a witch and could've put up quite a fight if she'd known what was about to happen.

"She put one of those silver straps on my wrists too, like the one she put on Zeb," Regina supplied, glancing at me. So the silver band, whatever it actually was, stripped Zeb and Regina of their powers, it seemed. She hadn't bothered to put one on my wrists, though. Interesting.

"Yeah, but not me. Weird." Mac shrugged.

"Alright. Girls, I know this is confusing, but we have to stay calm when she gets back. Can you do that for me?" I asked, looking between them. "We're going to figure this out. Just trust me." I glanced at Zeb, still motionless on the floor, his chest rising and falling with each breath. I had to figure out some way to wake him up and get that damned strap off his wrist.

I heard sounds outside the room then—shuffling footsteps and curses. Then a loud smack, like someone kicked something—a male voice; Aiden. "Fuck. It wasn't supposed to happen this way." Then I heard Essie in reply; muffled, so I couldn't make out her response.

Another crash. "Bullshit!" Aiden exclaimed.

The girls shuddered, and I braced myself as he flung the door open, striding into the small room with Essie in his wake.

"Cricket, how the fuck do you manage to stick your nose into all of my business?" He snarled at me, and I sensed his draconian aura; the metallic tang that hung in the air around him, thick and heavy as if it multiplied in accordance with his anger.

I glared back at him. "Maybe if your 'business' didn't include hurting my daughter and other people I love, I wouldn't have to stick my nose in it." When I overemphasized the word "business," I saw his jaw clench.

His phone dinged then, and he pulled it out of his pocket, scowling at it. He was dressed in a suit, which struck me as odd. A suit, in the wee hours of the morning, at an antique shop. And who was he texting with at this time of night? As he replaced the phone, I noticed a shiny flash of crimson and black hanging from his wrist—Essie's firestone. A plan started taking shape in my mind.

"Did you finally find what you were looking for, Aiden? The mysterious antique for your client? I'd love to take a look at it," I said, hoping to goad him into a response.

His icy gaze settled on me as he took a few steps forward and crouched down in front of me. "How nice of you to ask. I did, no thanks to you. And now I'm only hours away from getting out of this shithole and getting on with my life. If you play your cards right, maybe you'll make it out alive, too." He grinned, showing his pearly white teeth. I'd never noticed how straight and sharp they were until now.

Essie stood behind him, blankly staring straight ahead. My heart hurt for her. She didn't deserve to be used like this. What had happened here wasn't her fault; it was all Aiden's. I didn't hold her responsible. She was a victim, just like the rest of us were.

"Let her go, at least," I said, motioning to Essie with a nod of my head. "You've got us all here now. What else could you possibly need her for?"

"Don't you worry your pretty little head about it, Cricket." He booped me on the nose with his index finger before standing up. I rolled my eyes as my face flushed with anger. If only my hands were free, I could've made a grab for the firestone.

He walked over to Zeb, bent down, and checked the bindings on his wrists. "Such a shame I don't know where yours is..." he murmured as he slapped Zeb on the back before he stood up. Yes, a shame Aiden couldn't have two Reapers at his beck and call. And to think, Zeb had taken up for this guy.

He went over to Essie, who still stood immobile. Aiden brushed her cheek with his hand, looking deeply into her eyes. I watched as he placed a soft and brief kiss on her lips. I wanted to slap him.

Instead, I just yelled. "Stop it, Aiden! She trusted you!" Once again, I pulled on my bindings, but they held. I wasn't getting loose any time soon. Aiden ignored me but led Essie to the desk in the corner, seating her in the large cushioned chair.

He sighed and produced one of the silver straps from his coat pocket and wrapped it around Essie's wrists as the girls and I watched, all of us with bated breath. Then he pulled open a desk drawer and took out a roll of cording, just like what Essie had bound our hands with. He wrapped some of it around her wrists, tied it securely, then tucked her hair behind one ear. He stood back and looked at her. A soft smile came over his face as she gazed back at him with empty eyes.

Aiden shot me a hard glance, then stood there looking at Essie, rubbing his chin as if in thought. I cocked my head, waiting for his next move, when he held his wrist out and removed the firestone. He held it up by its chain, letting the light catch the crimson highlights. Essie blinked a few times as if regaining her consciousness. Her eyes found Aiden as he moved toward her.

"What's going on, Aiden?" she asked, her voice high pitched. He walked behind the chair and fastened the stone around her neck before she could move. She was free.

Mac watched with confusion written all over her face. Essie looked at the three of us, then at Zeb on the floor, her mouth falling open and her green eyes going wide.

"Aiden? What the hell?" she asked, gazing at him in horror. "Did you do this?"

"Actually, you did most of it." Mac glared at Essie, not realizing that she'd been under Aiden's control.

"Me?" Essie gasped, horrified. Her bound hands went to her throat, where they found the firestone hanging. She glanced accusingly at Aiden. "What did you do?"

I saw Aiden's Adam's apple bob as he swallowed. "I did what I had to do. I'm sorry it had to be like this." He looked around at all of us in turn, then focused on Essie again. "I really am."

I tried to think of a strategy. Essie was free from his

control now. Thank God. How could we use this to our advantage? *Think*.

Essie's eyes welled up with tears, staining her cheeks with black mascara as they spilled down her face. Aiden looked at the ceiling, not watching her break down. I wondered if he actually had feelings for her, deep down inside his black, selfish heart.

"After everything, Aiden? I helped you search for it. I welcomed you into my home—your father, too. I—" She glanced at the girls, who were watching intently as this drama unfolded. I assumed she was about to remind him of the nights of passion they'd spent together, and I silently thanked her for stopping herself.

"Essie. Don't." Aiden had the decency to look ashamed, at least. He stared at his feet now, shuffling them.

She was sobbing openly now, and my heart went out to her. None of this was her fault. She'd trusted the wrong guy and gotten hurt, like many of us have done. Only most of us didn't date a dragon shifter who was willing to throw us under the bus for power and fortune.

His phone dinged with another text, but he ignored it, moving closer to Essie. He ran his hands through his hair, then held on to the back of his neck as he approached the desk. He stood there for a moment, eyes closed, as she gasped between cries.

"Essie, I—" He dropped his hands to his sides.

She looked up at him with glistening eyes. "Can you at least let me go to the loo to wipe this shit off my face?"

He nodded, reaching for her elbow to help her up from the chair. She let him, then turned to face him as she stood. She held her wrists out.

"I need to use the loo," she said in explanation, expecting him to release the bindings.

He sighed and, to my astonishment, began working to undo the bindings around her wrists. I cut a glance at the girls and mouthed "shhh" to them.

He tossed the cording onto the desk and gestured toward an adjoining door that read "Restrooms," indicating she was free to go to the bathroom now. She sniffled and massaged her wrists, then examined the silver band on the right one.

"What's this about?" she asked, scowling at him and tugging at it. It didn't budge.

"You can pee with that on. Go on now, before I change my mind." He nodded toward the door again. Essie risked a glance at me as she started moving, and I nodded at her. This was her chance. She had to do something.

His phone chimed again as she closed the bathroom door behind her, and this time Aiden whipped it out of his pocket, perching himself on the corner of the desk to read the text.

We kept quiet, waiting to see what, if anything, Essie would do. After a couple of minutes, while Aiden sat on the desk, chuckling at whatever he was looking at on his phone, the door to the bathroom opened slowly. She caught my eye as she slid through the opening, putting one finger to her mouth.

I bit down on my lip, closed my eyes, and said a silent prayer. I opened my eyes again to see her creeping behind the desk where Aiden sat. I noticed the silver band was still on her wrist, and when she saw me looking at it, she shrugged.

Essie picked up a large paperweight from the desk and aimed it at Aiden's head when his phone chimed once again. Her eyes widened, and she smashed the paperweight against his head.

"Owww! What the fuck?" he asked, rubbing his head

and turning to look behind him. His phone fell to the ground, and the shock on his face was priceless when he saw Essie standing there with the paperweight. Before he could do anything, she punched him in the face, knocking him to the ground.

She rounded the desk and gave him a few good kicks to the stomach while he moaned and attempted to stand. She reached down, grabbing his collar, and drew her fist back with a snarl on her lips when a blast of flames shot through the doorway.

There was Stephan, in dragon form, breathing fire into the room. He growled, huffing and puffing as he advanced on Essie. The green and gold scales sparkled as he breathed fire, the light bouncing off of them. His wings flapped while his enormous body pushed through the doorway, nearly taking up the entire room. I struggled to stand, not knowing what I could do to help but feeling the need to try until Mac grabbed my arm and pulled me back down.

"MOM! What the hell is that?"

So much for keeping my daughter in the dark about the supernatural world.

"Just stay down!" I yelled, pulling away from her grasp so I could stand up.

Essie dropped Aiden, letting his head bounce off the floor while he yelled. She stood, defenseless against Stephan as I struggled to make it to her. The dragon snarled, smoky wisps trailing in the air around us, the door frame blackened and smoking from the flames he'd just breathed through it.

"Dad, stop! Stop it!" Aiden sat up, yelling and putting one hand up in the air. He held his head with the other one, wincing as he continued to yell for his dad to cease fire, literally.

Regina and Mac stared at the dragon with their jaws hanging open while Zeb was still undisturbed. I stood at Essie's side, ready to do whatever I could to help, when the dragon changed. I watched as the transformation took place, similar to what had happened at Essie's apartment when I'd met Stephan the first time.

Stephan's wings retracted, the scales faded away to reveal human skin beneath, his bones cracked and reshaped themselves as we watched. Stephan emerged from the dragon, in human form, right before our eyes. Wearing nothing but his own wrinkly skin, his gray hair slicked back and an ugly scowl on his face.

"Oh my God, ewww!" Mac cried, turning away. Regina covered her eyes with a gasp. I couldn't blame them. Stephan's physique wasn't exactly the statue of David.

Stephan scowled at us, looked around, and reached for a long coat that hung on a hook by the door. He put it on, then strode to where Essie and I still stood. She seemed stunned, but she thrust out one of her long legs in a roundhouse kick when he advanced on her. Stephan dodged, grabbed her ankle and twisted, bringing her to the ground with a thud and a hiss.

I made a move toward him, completely unsure of what I was doing but knowing I needed to try. He stomped on Essie's back while she was down, effectively incapacitating her as she screamed in pain. The girls huddled together, Mac whimpering and screaming for me to come back. Aiden was still down and staring at his father in disbelief, yelling for him to stop, when Stephan noticed me. A small smile played on his lips as he watched me heading toward him, which pissed me off. Maybe I was just a supernatural radar detector, but I could get a few good punches in, damn it.

He stood there, that stupid grin on his face, allowing me to approach. I drew back and backhanded him across the face as hard as I could with my hands bound, grunting with the impact. I bit back a scream of pain. Holy hell, that hurt. My entire left hand felt numb, and I shook them out, cursing, while Stephan tutted.

"Precious," he drawled, still smiling at me as if watching a baby taking their first steps. Then his face darkened, and he grabbed my hand, the one I'd just backhanded him with, and squeezed. I screamed. I couldn't help it. I felt bones crushing and colliding against one another inside my hand, and it brought me to my knees. I heard the girls screaming behind me while Essie still writhed in agony on the ground. Aiden stood up and was moved toward us, yelling for his dad to stop.

"DAD!" Aiden screamed louder, finally getting through to his father.

Stephan leveled his stony gaze at his own son, glaring at him and releasing me. I tumbled to the floor, and Mac and Regina gathered around me while I gasped and clutched my broken hand.

"How could you be so stupid? You gave her firestone back to her? I knew you were inept, but this mistake could've cost us everything."

Stephan leaned down, still glaring at Aiden, only glancing at Essie long enough to rip the cord from her neck, which held her firestone. He shoved it into the pocket of the coat he now wore.

"Tie her up again," he spat at Aiden, who jumped at his father's tone. Aiden took the length of binding from the desk and tied it around Essie's wrists again while glaring at his father. "I don't know why I trusted a boy to do a man's job."

Aiden glanced at him. A mixture of humiliation and anger swept across his face. "Maybe you should've done it yourself then, old man."

"Watch your tone. Not only am I your father, but I'm also your Elder."

Aiden's jaw clenched as he finished tying the bindings on Essie's wrists. She moaned in pain, her hands now tied behind her back, as she lay on the floor. I took deep breaths, trying to contain my nausea and push back the pain from my hand while also attempting to gauge the situation. Which seemed hopeless, now.

Stephan nodded at Aiden after he'd finished with Essie. "You—go to the car and retrieve it. I need to make sure it works before we leave."

Aiden spared a glance for us all, a hint of remorse in his eyes, before turning to do as he was told.

Stephan's eyes landed on me, and he shook his head. "You're more trouble than you're worth. All you damned Revealers, every last one of ya." He snarled at me, and my head shot up at that last remark.

'All you damned Revealers'? He knew others like me? Who were they? Where were they? I desperately wanted to know, but the pain in my hand and my anger at him kept me quiet—for now.

"What's he talking about, Mom?" Mac asked me in a whisper. I exchanged a look with Regina and sighed, meeting Mac's gaze.

"That's a conversation for later, Mac. I'll explain, I promise." I reached for her hand with my good one and gave it a squeeze. She drew her perfectly drawn brows together and pursed her lips, then nodded.

Stephan walked the room, examining books and antiques as he went, knocking some to the floor with a grunt of disgust. I racked my brain, trying to come up with a plan while we waited for Aiden and whatever it was he had gone to fetch for his father.

The more I thought, the more hopeless it seemed. Zeb was out cold, Essie was in worse shape than she'd been when we arrived, and now Aiden had his father here to help keep us all in check. There was nothing we could do at this point except hope for a change in our favor as things progressed.

Aiden came back in, carrying a trunk which he placed on the floor beside his dad. Regina and Mac gasped simultaneously.

"That's ours!"

"How did you get that?"

The girls stared at him as Stephan rummaged through the contents of the trunk. He tossed out clothing, hats, and other ephemera until he finally pulled out a leather-bound book. He handled it carefully, as if it were the most precious thing on the planet, then turned to us with a devious grin.

"You ladies had the good fortune of stumbling across this chest full of treasures before my bumbling idiot of a son could find it," Stephan explained, giving Aiden a disdainful glance. "That one has been wearing the ring. That's how we knew you'd found it," he said, nodding at Mac, who clasped one hand over the other one, which held the ring.

"So, the item you've been searching for was in the chest?" I asked, wanting to keep the conversation going, hoping he'd become careless and provide us an opening for escape. I didn't watch every season of "Criminal Minds" for nothing.

He eyed me as if sensing my ulterior motive but continued talking. "It was. Although the trunk held much greater treasures than I could've ever hoped for." He held the book up again, carefully opening it. He studied the page for a moment, then brought his gaze up to mine, closing the book again.

"That emerald ring holds special powers, but only for those with dormant abilities already." I swung my gaze to Mac, whose mouth was hanging open. "Your daughter seems to have... some abilities. Although I'm not sure if she's a Revealer like you or something else. She seemed to subconsciously fight the power of the ring, never using its full potential."

My mind raced back to when Regina had visited me and warned me that Mac was acting weird. I remembered a few instances of her temper flaring and her strange behavior. I had chalked it up to teenage angst, but had it been the ring? What ability could she have if she wasn't a Revealer like me? Regina grabbed hold of Mac's hand while Mac shook, staring at Stephan and the book he held.

He eyed me carefully, then smirked. "You didn't know, did you?"

I didn't want to answer, and luckily I didn't have to.

"What's that book you've got there? I don't remember seeing it in the trunk." Regina, brave girl that she was, asked. She squared her jaw and met his gaze head-on. This girl had taken on a vampire by herself once before, but I was still impressed that she was willing to jump right into the frying pan with Stephan.

Aiden spoke up then, rubbing the back of his neck sheepishly. "There was a false bottom. It was under there."

Stephan scowled at him, then turned back to Regina. "Funny you should ask. You're the witch, right? Descended from the Caveden line?"

Mac gawked at her friend while Regina seemed

unphased. "Why should I tell you anything?" Regina narrowed her eyes at him.

"Because this is your family grimoire, passed down for generations, only to be lost for the last hundred years." He held the book out so Regina could get a look at it. "And now we have it and a Caveden witch to go with it."

"Wait, what are you getting at?" I asked, glancing from Regina to Stephan.

A devious smile played on Stephan's lips. "This book contains spells that only a Caveden witch can perform. Spells that can fulfill my wildest dreams, making our Clutch the most powerful in the world, and me the most powerful Elder." Aiden cocked his head at his father at the words "my wildest dreams."

"And why would I want to perform those spells for you?" Regina asked, rolling her perfectly smoked eyes at him. I felt sure she would've tossed her black curls over her shoulder had her wrists not been bound together.

"Because you seem to be the type of young lady who would care what happens to her family. Maybe her brother, Robbie."

Regina's demeanor changed instantly. Her eyes grew wide as she asked, "What have you done to him?"

We had met Robbie briefly when my vampire boss, Nina, had forced me to help her find a cure for her mortality curse. It turned out that her lover slash stepson, Aaron, and Robbie were secret lovers, and Robbie had found the cure just in time to save Aaron's life, but not Nina's. The two lovers had run off together after Aaron took the vial containing the cure, and as far as I knew, Regina and her mother hadn't heard from Robbie or Aaron since then.

"Agree to help me, and he stays safe. If not..." Stephan

allowed his eyes to spark, reminding us of his true form and what he was capable of.

Regina looked at me for help, but there was nothing we could do. Not yet, anyway. I said another silent prayer for a miracle to happen, and soon.

"Now, I want you to perform a small spell from the book, just to confirm we've traced your line correctly. Let's have a little fun, shall we?" he asked with a sinister smile, rubbing his hands together.

A cold chill washed over me at his last words. I took in our situation again—Essie, lying face down on the floor, hands bound behind her back and the silver strap still on her arm. Also, Stephan had her firestone and could reclaim control over her at any moment. Zeb was still down for the count. I didn't know what they'd done to him, but whatever it was, he was out cold. Regina, Mac, and I had our wrists bound, and Regina had a silver strap on hers, which eliminated her powers as well.

Wait. Mac and I didn't have silver straps on our wrists. Aiden hadn't bothered with us, thinking Mac was completely human and that I had no powers that could be used against them as a Revealer. Stephan was unaware of that detail. Sadly, Aiden was probably right, though; I couldn't think of anything I could do that would be useful. I tried to remember everything I'd read and studied about Revealers. There had to be something else I could do, something I could use to help us. Hadn't Gus mentioned something about my abilities possibly "evolving"? Well, I could use some evolution right about now, damn it.

Stephan leafed through the book, holding it in one hand. He stopped on a page about halfway through and ran his finger down it, murmuring and nodding. "This. Let's try this one. Bring the witch, Son, and remove her bracelet."

I saw Aiden's jaw working as he made his way over to Regina. She recoiled from him, but he grabbed her by the elbows and pulled her to her feet. Swiftly removing the silver band around her wrists, he gave her a little shove toward his father.

"Watch it!" I yelled at him. He and Stephan ignored me, all of their attention focused on Regina.

"This one should be simple enough for you to handle. Then we'll try something a little more complicated." Stephan put the book within Regina's line of sight, and after an anxious glance at me, she read it. "And no funny business, you hear?"

She ignored him. "You want me to levitate someone?" She squinted her eyes at the book.

"Yes, but not just anyone. The unconscious Reaper over there." He nodded toward Zeb, whose chest rose and fell in a peaceful rhythm, oblivious to everything happening around him.

"Why?" I asked. What the hell was Stephan up to? And Regina was now free, but would she be brave enough to do anything to help us?

"Nobody pulled your chain, Mrs. Jones." Stephan's icy gaze slid over to where Zeb lay. "Aiden, take the bracelet off him."

Aidan scoffed. "You just called me an idiot for giving Essie's firestone back to her. Now you want both of their bracelets off?"

Stephan strode over to where Aiden stood, getting right up in his son's face. "Yes. Do you have a problem with that?"

Aiden stood up a bit taller. "Actually, I do. Why the hell should I take his bracelet off? He's a stronger Reaper than she is. It would be an enormous risk if he woke up without it."

I watched with interest, hoping Aiden would do it. At least without the "bracelet," as they called it, Zeb would be able to do something to help us if he woke up, even if Regina couldn't.

"He won't. Now, do it."

Aidan shook his head but walked over to Zeb and did as he was told. He bent down and slipped the silver band from Zeb's wrists, tucking it into his own pocket with Regina's.

"Happy?" he asked his father, stepping away from Zeb.

Stephan ignored him and motioned for Regina. "Do it. Let's see what you've got."

Regina rolled her eyes and sighed. Mac's gaze was locked on her friend. I glanced toward Zeb, still motionless.

"This won't hurt him?" I asked, not directing it at anyone in particular.

Regina smiled softly at me. "No, it won't hurt him." I nodded, saying a prayer that it would wake him up instead.

With a last look of disdain at Stephan, Regina took another look at the book, then started to chant the words. It sounded like a mixture of Latin and Greek to me, rolling from her lips as if it were her native tongue. With a few gestures of her hands, she looked at Zeb, and then he was rising off the floor. She stared at him, still chanting and raising her hands higher as he continued to climb higher as well.

When Zeb was a good three feet off the floor, Stephan clapped his hands, grinning from ear to ear. "Yes! And that was just the warm up! Put him down. Let's do one more."

Regina scowled but lowered her arms, repeating the foreign words while Zeb lowered back to the floor, still unconscious and limp. *Damn it.*

Stephan clasped Regina's shoulder, still grinning, and she shook him off. "Are we done?" she asked.

"Done? We're just getting started, darlin'," he said, picking up the book from the desk again.

Regina gave me a withering glance, then I noticed her gaze settle on Mac, who stared in disbelief at her friend. Regina mouthed "sorry" and shrugged, but Mac didn't respond.

"Now, how about.... this one." Stephan flipped a few pages, then tapped the page he landed on. He held it out for Regina to read.

She shook her head. "Are you insane? No." She jutted her chin out defiantly, and I was proud of her but also frightened of Stephan's reaction to her refusal.

He glared at her. "Think carefully before you tell me no. We wouldn't want to disappoint Robbie, would we?" He raised an eyebrow at her, standing there looking ridiculous in a long coat and nothing else, yet terrifying as hell.

Regina's eyes welled with tears. She spun around to look at Mac and me helplessly.

"Dad, let's just go, alright? We know she's the one." Aiden said, rubbing his jaw. He glanced at Essie, still lying quietly, hands bound behind her back, mascara streaks running down her cheeks.

"What's the spell?" I asked. I hadn't forgotten that Aiden had neglected to put the silver band back on Zeb's wrist; maybe this spell Stephan wanted her to do could wake Zeb up somehow.

"It's a Cruciamentum curse," Regina stated. "To inflict excruciating pain."

Oh.

She turned back to Stephan. "I'm not doing it!" she yelled at him.

Stephan's face twisted, his eyes flickering. He began to change, but not completely. His face contorted, taking on the shape of a dragon's with an elongated mouth and wide, flaring nostrils. His eyes glinted as they transformed. He looked like a grotesque science experiment, standing there with his human body draped in a gaping, long coat, with the head of a dragon sitting atop it. He exhaled a streak of flames in Regina's direction, eliciting a yelp from her. He came closer, flames flaring and retreating from his jaws with each breath he took.

"Stop! She can do the spell on me!" I yelled. "STOP!"

"Mom!" Mac cried, clutching my arm.

Half-dragon Stephan nodded in my direction, then morphed back into his full human form, bones and cartilage crunching as he did. Regina whimpered, holding her head in her hands, which were still bound at the wrist, while she shook.

"How generous of you to offer, Mrs. Jones," Stephan drawled after his transformation was complete. Regina continued to cry, shaking her head at me, while Mac was holding on to me as best she could with her wrists bound.

My crushed hand still throbbed with every heartbeat, making it hard to concentrate. I had to do this, no matter how painful it would be. I couldn't let him torture Regina any longer or hurt Robbie.

"Let's do this," I said. Mac squeezed my arm, and I turned to her, whispering, "It'll be okay. Don't worry." I mustered a tiny smile for her and saw her face relax a bit, then I turned to Regina.

"It's alright, Regina. Go ahead."

I smiled at her encouragingly, and she dragged the back of her hand across her face, wiping her tears away. She sent an icy stare in Stephan's direction, who stood watching in amusement. Aiden was edging his way around the desk, and I wondered what he was up to.

Regina read from the book as Stephan held it in front of her. Again, the strange words sounded like a melody leaving her lips, beautiful and rhythmic. I was being lulled into a peaceful state, just listening to her speak, when I felt the first stab of pain slice through my head. Instinctively, I grabbed at my head with my hands bound, then doubled over as another surge of pain slammed into my gut.

I was on my knees, feeling like I was being torn apart from the inside out when I heard a high-pitched keening sound and realized it was coming from me. I fell to the floor, shaking and twisting, as wave after wave of pain hit me. Mac screamed as Regina continued to chant, tears streaming down her cheeks. Stephan laughed, clapping his hands as he watched me writhing in pain.

"Enough, Dad!" Aiden yelled.

Stephan scowled at his son for a moment. "STOP!" he bellowed.

Regina stopped her chanting immediately and rushed to my side, sobbing. The pain began to subside almost instantly, and I felt better with each second that passed.

"I'm so sorry," Regina cried, gently putting her hand on my arm.

A sadistic smile came over his face. "Very good, Ramona," he drawled, not even getting her name right. "I think it's time we headed home now. We got what we came for—and more. Son, put the trunk back in the car. I'll bring the witch out shortly."

My head whipped around, "What did you say?"

Stephan glared at me. "The witch is coming with us."

Aiden sighed heavily, scratching his well-defined jaw. I caught the almost imperceptible glance he threw Essie, then noticed that she seemed to be in a slightly different position than before. But how could that be? My recently tortured brain was probably just playing tricks on me.

"Yeah... we're not doing that, Dad." Aidan raised an eyebrow at his dad and crossed his arms. "You didn't say anything about the witch being a teenager before, and I'm not going down for kidnapping a minor."

Stephan narrowed his eyes at his son, his cold gaze making goosebumps appear on my skin, even though it wasn't me he glared at. "I don't know how I ended up with such a weakling for a son," he said through gritted teeth.

Aiden's face flushed at the words, and his fists clenched at his sides. "Weak? I've done everything you've ever asked of me, even when I didn't agree with it. You've finally let power drive you mad though. You're gonna drive our Clutch into the ground. This completely crosses the line, and I won't have any part of it, Dad."

He'd no sooner finished speaking when Stephan slapped him. A red mark started forming on his flesh immediately and Aiden lifted a hand to his face, which had to be stinging.

A sardonic half-smile crept over Aiden's face as he said, "You're not fit to be Elder anymore. I'm telling the Council everything when we get back. About this trip, the grimoire, the witch... all of it." His smile widened as he met his father's gaze, still holding his face. "It's over."

"Watch your mouth, boy. Maybe you shouldn't come back at all. Maybe you belong here, playing house with your little girlfriend." Stephan sneered, reaching for Regina's arm. Aidan stepped toward his dad, but Stephan reached out and took Aiden's wrist, twisting it until I heard bones cracking. Aiden cried out, but Stephan kept twisting, a sick smile on his face as he watched his son fall to his knees.

Aiden was on the floor, moaning when Stephan finally

let go. Aiden's shoulder appeared to be dislocated, and his face contorted into a grimace.

"Come on, witch," he said to Regina, taking her roughly by the elbow while she recoiled. Stephan's gaze passed over me. An evil grin crept over his features as he said to Mac, "You too, baby Revealer. Or whatever you are."

15

M ac's eyes widened. She turned to me with a look of desperation. "Mom..." she said, and I felt the fear radiating from her. I stood up, aching all over, my ruined hand still bound to the other one, hanging in front of me. I felt like an eighteen-wheeler had run me over, but I'd be damned if he was taking my daughter or Regina out of here.

"Think again, Komodo asshole. Neither of these girls is going anywhere with you. Not happening." I stepped in front of Mac, and I grabbed Regina's other elbow and pulled her back toward me and away from Stephan. Blood rushed to my cheeks, my heart raced. No way in hell was this happening. Over my dead body.

The older man glared at me, his eyes sparking, indicating he was probably about to shift. Fear threatened to take hold, but I pushed it back and focused on my anger instead. How dare he come here and think he could force Regina, and now my daughter, to go with him back to Atlanta to do his bidding?

I saw a movement from the corner of my eye, but I kept

my eyes focused on Stephan. Essie moved first one leg, then the other, slowly rising up behind Stephan. Aiden, having calmed considerably, still held his dislocated shoulder but nodded at Essie as she caught his eye. I reminded myself not to look directly at her. I didn't want to give Stephan a heads up that she was about to attack.

Her hands were free now, apparently thanks to Aiden removing the bindings while Regina had been inflicting fifty-seven different kinds of pain on me with the spell. I stood still, allowing him to advance on me as Essie crept up behind him.

"I had decided to allow you to live, vile Revealer that you are. But I don't think I will. The only good Revealer is a dead one," he spat at me, and I recoiled. What the hell did I not know about Revealers that made us "vile"? I made a mental note to have a long talk with Gus later.

I was forming a response when Essie quickly looped her arm around Stephan's neck and pulled him to her, choking him. He was taken completely by surprise, his eyes widening and his hands trying to pry her arm off of his neck.

She tightened again, hauling him off his feet. "That's for using my firestone against me." She tugged again, and Stephan sputtered and coughed, frantically grabbing at her arm. "That's for treating your own son like shit." She twisted again, her lovely features contorting into a snarl. "And that's for messing with the people I love."

While Essie dealt out some much-needed karma, Aiden crept toward Zeb. There was a small vial of clear liquid in his hand, and while Essie had his father occupied, Aiden leaned down and tilted Zeb's head back, pouring the liquid into Zeb's mouth. Then Aiden removed the bindings from Zeb's wrists and placed him back on the ground. Aiden saw me watching him, and he gave me a nod which I didn't return. I didn't trust him yet, even if he was helping us at the moment.

Stephan jabbed an elbow into Essie's ribs, and she staggered away, losing her grip on his neck and the element of surprise. He turned his full attention on Aiden, realizing what his son had done. His eyes darkened, his nostrils flared, and his mouth twisted into an ugly snarl.

"You've made it clear whose side you're on, Son."

Stephan reached into his coat pocket, pulling out Essie's firestone and smirking. "Luckily, I still have this." He held it up as if to admire it, and Essie looked at Aiden with a silent plea. Wasting no time, Aiden tackled his dad, sending the firestone skidding across the room and underneath a large antique hutch. I breathed a sigh of relief as I watched it disappear out of reach.

Father and son were brawling now, rolling around on the floor, throwing punches wherever they could land one. They grunted and groaned as they fought for control while the girls and I stayed as far back as we could. Something drew my eye as we watched them, and I let my gaze follow it. Zeb was moving! Essie rushed to his side, helping him stand. He took in the surrounding scene with wide eyes, his gaze landing on mine momentarily. I couldn't read his look for sure, but it seemed to be a mixture of remorse and shock. I looked away as he got to his feet and jumped into the melee.

It was two Reapers and Aiden against Stephan now, and as the fighting resumed, I caught the distinct crackle and dry heat in the air of the Reapers auras and saw the shimmering airwaves surrounding the dragon shifters. Essie and Zeb's super strength, high speed, and stamina kicked in as they delivered punches and kicks to Stephan's shifting form.

While he transformed into his draconian form, Aiden did too. I'd never seen him as a dragon before. I only sensed his aura and knew he was a dragon. As frightened as I was, I had to admit it was a sight to see, watching these two shift into their larger dragon forms.

Bones crunched and reshaped themselves, both of them growing larger and larger while the room grew smaller and smaller. Iridescent scales grew over human flesh, and wings sprouted on their backs. Tails swished back and forth, clearing anything in their path. The girls and I flattened ourselves against the back wall, trying to stay out of their way as the two dragons went head to head, breathing fire and smoke at each other. The mossy green and gold dragon was Stephan, who aimed his fiery breath at the other three. Aiden, a burnished rust and gold-colored dragon, was a little smaller than his father but fierce all the same. He growled, throwing his head back and baring his teeth, then emitted a wave of flames at his father, who howled at the impact.

Stephan's tail swished, knocking a hole in the wall opposite us, nearly taking out the entire partition. The house creaked and moaned, and I wondered if the structure would fall in on top of us. The girls screamed, shook, and clung to me while we tried to make ourselves as invisible as possible. The three of us still had our hands bound, but Regina no longer had the silver strap. I turned to face her, grasping her arm.

"Regina, can you cast a spell? Anything you think could help? Can you try?" I asked, speaking loudly to be heard over the noise of the dragons roaring.

"I—I don't know. I'll try," she said, brows creased in a frown. I knew she was scared and also racked with guilt over being forced to use the pain spell on me earlier. It would be hard for her to concentrate with the supernatural smack-down going on right under our noses, but I prayed she could do something to help.

She closed her eyes and began chanting in the strange mix of Latin and Greek words, so I turned to Mac to see how she was doing. I smiled at her and pushed her hair back away from her tear-streaked face.

"This is not how I wanted you to find out, sweetie." I brushed her cheek. Tears welled in my eyes as I looked at her. My baby, practically grown up now. She was sixteen, driving, and now she'd have to face some hard truths about who she was. This wasn't fair, and it wasn't what I wanted for her.

She put on a brave face for me, pursed her lips, then said, "We're gonna be okay, right, Mom?"

I nodded, a few tears sliding down my cheeks. "We're gonna be okay."

I squeezed her hand and turned back to see Regina still trying to do something to help, with little effect. "Where's the book?" she asked me. "I need that pain spell again!"

I glanced around the room, everything in disarray. Antiques, broken and bent, lying everywhere, papers scattered on the floor, books flung to every corner of the room. I spotted the book and made a dash for it while Stephan was distracted. I brought it back to Regina, who flipped through the pages until she found what she was looking for.

She chanted again, focusing on Stephan, and I felt the heat and energy radiating from her. Stephan halted and stiffened, obviously feeling the effects of Regina's spell. He threw his great head back and growled, so loud the walls of the tiny shop quaked. His body twisted in agony as he moaned and growled, his eyes rolling back in his head while the others continued to assault him as well.

It was working! I turned to Regina, grinning from ear to ear, only to see her on the brink of exhaustion. My smile faded as I realized this spell was clearly taking everything out of her. Sweat glistened on her forehead, and a small stream of blood ran from one nostril. Her eyes grew heavy, and she faltered as she chanted.

"Regina! Sweetie, keep going if you can, you're doing it!" I yelled to her, knowing she couldn't hold it for much longer. I feared we had only succeeded in pissing Stephan off more and that we would pay for this attempt to thwart him later.

Regina opened her eyes and gave me a weary look, then whispered, "I'm sorry." She slumped to the floor. Mac caught her as best as she could with her wrists still bound.

"Mom, what now?" Mac asked, her voice cracking on the words. I didn't know how to respond.

Stephan was regaining his strength and landed a blow with his tail that sent Essie skidding across the room and into the desk in the corner with a resounding thud. He roared and sent a stream of flames toward Zeb, who recoiled, smoke rolling off his clothing where the flames licked at him. Then in one fluid motion, Stephan had his son's dragon form on the floor, with one enormous foot on top of him. He growled, roared, and sputtered flames while Aiden did the same. I wondered if they were having some sort of Draconian conversation?

Then both of them began to transform back into their respective human forms, the scales and wings receding into human flesh once again. Mac averted her gaze from the two naked men now standing before us, and I tried to at least avoid looking at their nether regions.

Stefan stooped to pick up the coat he'd been wearing before, donning it once again. Everyone else was down for the count and licking their wounds. It seemed Stephan may have won this round, but I'd be damned if I'd let him win the battle.

Stephan walked over to Essie and yanked her up by the hair as she yelped. He practically dragged her to the center of the room by her hair, then dropped her. She tumbled to the floor with a groan.

"This is the problem, Son. You fell in love, and now your loyalties have been compromised. I can't count on you any longer." He curled his wrinkled face up into a scowl as he spoke. "You're no son of mine," he hissed. He stomped on Essie's back, driving his heel into her flesh as she screamed.

Zeb rushed him, taking him down to the ground, where they wrestled until Stephan finally landed a blow to Zeb's head. He faltered only for a moment, but it was long enough. Stephan slapped one of the silver straps on Zeb's wrist again, then pulled him into a chokehold. He twisted just enough to pinch Zeb's carotid arteries, and then Zeb was out like a light.

Stephan strode back over to Essie, still writing in pain, and slapped a silver strap on her wrist as well. He then took a length of it, wrapped her wrists with it, binding them behind her back and tying it securely. He kicked her in the side.

Aiden, still nude, lunged at him, but Stephan was ready for him. He caught his son in a headlock, twisting Aiden's head to force him to look at Essie. "Look at her! I'll kill her. Do you hear me? I'll do it right now unless you help me get the hell out of here with what I came for, then you can go fuck yourself for all I care." He tossed Aiden to the side, then strode over to Essie, pulling her up by her black-streaked platinum blonde hair again. She cried out, then whimpered while struggling against him. Mac and I stood huddled in the corner near Regina's prone body.

Stephan's malicious grin grew wider as he held Essie there, the other hand poised in front of her throat. His hand transformed into the dragon's, claws appearing where his fingers once were, long and sharp. He ran one of them across Essie's neck, drawing a thin line of blood.

"Aiden…" she moaned softly, her voice weak.

"Stop it, Dad. Just stop." Aiden ran a hand through his short hair, his eyes trained on Essie's.

"Put the trunk and the witch in the car. Now," Stephan barked. Aiden hesitated, but when Stephan brought his claws closer to Essie's neck again, he threw his hands up in the air. He retrieved the trunk, placing the old grimoire inside before closing it. He picked it up, glaring at his father, then strode out of the room with it.

"You're not taking Regina." My voice came out strong and bold, with much more confidence than I felt. My hands shook, so I curled them into fists to stop them from giving me away.

"It's not up to you." Stephan didn't even bother to look at me. He turned Essie's head back and forth, still grasping her hair, teasing her neck with his claw.

Aiden came back into the room, wearing pants and without the trunk, giving his father a murderous look. "Let her go."

"Soon enough. Take the witch to the car, and I'll take the other one. Then I don't give a damn what you do."

Mac's grip on my arm tightened, and I said, "I told you, you're not taking Regina or my daughter anywhere."

He dropped Essie into a heap on the floor then, coming to stand directly in front of me. "And I told you I'll do what I damn well please," he said through gritted teeth. His cold, hard eyes bored into mine as if to challenge me.

I felt something ignite within me, shooting a fiery

current through my veins. My entire body vibrated with rage, and the only thought pulsing in my brain was to stop Stephan at any cost.

He reached out and took my daughter by the arm, jerking her roughly toward him. And that was it. My memories came flooding back to me of the night I passed out in Essie's apartment. I felt something physically snap inside of me. I raised my hands up in front of myself with them still bound at the wrists. Energy rose inside of me, coursing through my limbs, concentrating in my hands. His ugly snarl threw more gasoline on the fire of my anger, and I watched incredulously as a ball of light formed between my palms. I felt a burning desire to hurl it at Stephan. There was nothing I wanted more in this world.

So, I did.

16

Beep. Beep. Beep. The monotonous tone reverberated in my head, over and over. I opened my eyes to find myself, once again, in a hospital room. An IV was attached to my arm and the machine making the hateful beeping sound was monitoring my heart rate. I looked down to find one of my arms in a cast up to my elbow. My head throbbed with scenes from the antique shop.

The girls! Where were they? I was alone in my room. Where was everyone? I saw a dim light coming from underneath what appeared to be the bathroom door, so I called out. "Hello?"

Shuffling sounds came from behind the door, then Mac came bounding out, rushing to the side of my bed.

"Mom!" She threw herself onto the bed with me, hugging me tightly. I grimaced but laughed and hugged her back.

"Are you okay, Mac? Let me see," I said, cupping her cheek. She released me and held her arms out for me to inspect her.

She smiled softly. "See? I'm fine. So is Regina."

Thank God. I had been about to ask about Mac's best friend. "She is? That's great news! What about everyone else? Where are they?" I sat up in my bed, despite the pain it caused.

"Essie is recovering at her apartment. Apparently, Reapers heal super fast. She and Zeb are doing fine," Mac said, then looked away. My girl was smart. She knew something was up.

The mere mention of his name crushed my heart, threatening to shatter it into a million pieces. I loved him, sure, but was love enough? Could it overcome the feelings of distrust, disbelief, and disapproval I'd felt from him for so long now? Maybe he was feeling the same way I was and wondering if our relationship had run its course? I shook my head to clear those thoughts away. There would be time for that later.

"And Stephan? Tell me what happened."

Her eyes lit up as she started telling me. "Mom, you took him down! All by yourself. It was amazing!"

I chuckled. "I did? What did I do?"

"You don't remember? After all the fighting was over, he was about to take Regina and me away, and you stopped him. You stood there in front of him, and your face got all red, and you looked super angry. Then this ball of light shot out of your hands and blasted into him!" she exclaimed, the words tumbling out of her while she looked thoroughly impressed with her mother's supernatural prowess.

I sucked in a mouthful of air. I did that? It seemed vaguely familiar now that she mentioned it. I recalled feeling more rage than I'd ever felt before in my life. It seemed to take over my entire being. Had my Revealer senses evolved like Gus had suggested? I had to admit, the thought both terrified and also intrigued me.

"Did I—Is he..." I wanted to know if I had killed Stephan, but I also *didn't* want to know if I had killed him.

"He's not dead, but he's critical. He's in the ICU here, and the doctors and nurses are all talking about how he must've been hit by one hell of a bolt of lightning." She laughed and rolled her eyes. "Either way, I'm still calling you the Dragon Slayer."

I playfully punched her arm with my good hand. "Don't you dare!" I giggled. "Cricket, the Dragon Slayer" had a nice ring to it, though.

"What about Aiden?" I asked. I wasn't sure how to feel about him. He'd had ulterior motives the entire time. But in the end, when it really mattered, he'd come through for us and helped thwart his father. I didn't think we could've done it if he hadn't released Essie and Zeb, and no matter what my personal feelings were toward him, I would feel grateful for his last-minute change of heart.

Her expression darkened. "He's gone. I spoke to Essie— he left her a note. He apologized for using her and said he hadn't planned to fall in love with her, but he did. He was ashamed of himself and said he didn't deserve her, so he couldn't stay. That's mostly why she's been holed up in her apartment, recovering from a broken heart."

I frowned. Poor Essie. According to Zeb, she'd had nothing but bad luck in the love department, and now this had to happen. I was sure she was overcome with guilt over her part in all of this too, even though it wasn't her fault.

"Wonders never cease. I'm a little proud of him for owning up to his actions." I took Mac's hand and squeezed.

"Hold that thought. He took the trunk, including the

grimoire, with him when he left," Mac said, shrugging. "Everything is gone, except this ring." She held up her hand where the green-stoned ring was still on her finger.

"That's the Aiden we all know and hate."

"Anyway," she continued, "after you blasted Stephan, you collapsed, and then Gus and Joey arrived. Joey insisted you needed to go to the hospital." She pursed her lips, trying to suppress a smile. She was too smart for her own good, that one.

"Wait. How did they know we were there?"

She shrugged again. "I'm not sure. Gus said he'd explain everything to you later, though."

"Alright, well, go get a nurse for me because I need to get out of here." I examined the needle in my arm and considered ripping it out myself. "Where are my clothes?"

"Mom, slow down! I'll go get a nurse. Just chill," she said, a frown settling on her pretty face. She flipped her black hair over her shoulder as she rose from my bed.

"Hey, Mac?"

She turned around, rolling her eyes. "What?"

"I love you. And we're going to figure it all out, okay?"

She pressed her lips together, and tears welled in her emerald eyes. "Okay. I love you too."

Mac opened the door to my room, and Zeb was there, holding a gigantic bouquet of roses and his hand poised to knock.

"Oh, hey. I was just... yeah," Mac said, then squeezed past him. Zeb chuckled, a look of amusement on his face as he watched her make her escape. He turned his gaze to me, his blazing sapphire eyes turning serious as he approached.

"Princess," he whispered, leaning down to kiss my cheek. He sat the roses on the side table and shoved his hands into his pockets. He looked no worse for wear, aside from his blond hair being a little more disheveled than usual. He wore a flannel, jeans, and his black-rimmed glasses, and he rubbed at the stubble on his jawline as he stood, waiting for me to say something.

"I'm glad you're okay, Zeb," I said to break the awkward silence. The tension was thick in the air between us, almost forming a tangible barrier. I looked down at my cast, where Mac had already taken the liberty of writing "Dragon Slayer" in purple ink. *Great.*

"Cricket, I'm sorry. I'm sorry I didn't believe your hunch about Aiden and that I brushed aside all your concerns. The bloke fooled us—fooled me, anyway. I've been a right gobshite, and I'm sorry." He gave me a weak half-smile, his eyes hopeful.

I looked away from him, examining the blanket over my lap. I ran my fingers over the texture of the knit fabric, feeling the twists and knots the yarn formed. I wasn't quite sure what to say, but I gathered my thoughts as quickly as possible. There was no putting it off now. "It really hurt me that you chose to believe Aiden instead of me. I thought we were supposed to have each other's backs, no matter what. It was disappointing." I spoke softly and slowly, weighing each word as I said it.

He moved to sit on the bed with me, taking my hand, and I let him. "I do. I do have your back, always. It was a lapse in judgment. I wish I could do it all over again. I'd listen to you this time."

I chewed on the inside of my lip. "Zeb, I'm just really confused right now. You were so focused on Essie and her happiness, hell-bent on Aiden being the best thing to ever happen to her. You lost focus on me—on us. I'm not sure where to go from here."

His smile faltered as he looked down at my hand he was

still holding, then met my eyes again. "I get it. We have to work on us now. No distractions."

I sighed, feeling fresh tears welling in my eyes. "I think I have to work on me for a bit, Zeb."

Silence for a few beats, and then, "What are you saying?"

"I need some time."

His brow furrowed as he brought my hand to his lips, brushing a kiss against my knuckles. "Cricket..." His eyes glistened as they met mine. A few tears rolled down my cheeks as I looked at him and saw the pain and remorse in his eyes. It would be so easy to just say all was forgiven and move on as if nothing ever happened. As if he had never hurt me.

But he did.

And I wasn't that girl anymore who spent so many years trapped in a marriage that didn't work, forgiving him for the same things over and over again. Being the only one who tried, the only one who cared about holding things together. The woman I had become looked out for herself and didn't accept anything less than what she deserved.

"I need some time," I repeated. I didn't want to say I was sorry because I wasn't. I didn't have anything to be sorry for.

He nodded, squeezing my hand. "Alright, if you need time, take it. I'll still be here whenever you're ready." He stood, releasing my hand and cupping my face with his. He brought his lips to mine in a soft, lingering kiss, caressing my cheek with his thumb.

He backed away, and with a last look, he left. And I sat in my hospital bed and cried.

AFTER BEING RELEASED from the hospital, I spent a couple of days moping around the house, listening to sad songs, and drinking excessive amounts of vodka. Zeb had cleared all of his things out of my side of the duplex before I was released and had settled back in on his side. I was careful not to run into him when leaving the house or checking the mail. I wasn't ready for that kind of awkwardness yet.

On Friday, I decided I'd wallowed for long enough. It was time to rejoin society, and I would do just that with a trip to Forever Young to visit Grandma and Gus. I'd also be able to get some information I needed from Gus while I was there, which would kill two birds with one stone. I wasn't sure how much Grandma knew about recent developments, but I wanted to see her. Sometimes a girl just needed a hug.

"Cricket!" Grandma greeted me at the door of her apartment inside the assisted living facility with that hug I'd been craving. I squeezed her back, taking in the sweet scent of her Japanese cherry blossom lotion and body spray. Tears sprang to my eyes, but I held them back. I didn't want her to see them.

Grandma's gaze landed on my cast, which I'd done my best to conceal with a long-sleeved cardigan. At least the words "Dragon Slayer" that Mac had scrawled on it was hidden from view. Her eyes widened. "What happened to you?"

"Hey, Grandma... Gus," I greeted them, stepping inside the apartment as Grandma held the door open for me. "Oh, this?" I held my arm out as Grandma's hands flew to her mouth. "I tripped on the stairs at the duplex and fell. Just a little cracked bone, nothing to worry about. I'll be good as new in no time. So... how's the puzzle-making going?" I asked, trying to change the subject.

Gus scowled at me. "It's going."

"He's still working on my special puzzle! I just know it's gonna be a dandy!" she exclaimed, clapping her hands together while Gus rolled his eyes in annoyance. I stifled a giggle by pressing my lips together.

"Are you sure you're okay, Cricket?" Gus asked, glancing at my cast and then meeting my gaze again. I knew he was asking about more than just my arm. We needed to talk, and we needed to distract Grandma.

"I'm feeling better now. My stomach was upset from the pain meds for a couple of days, and I couldn't eat much. But I think I could just about eat a horse now, though." I glanced at Grandma, hoping she'd take the bait.

"Why didn't you call me? I could've taken care of you! Let me make you a sandwich!" Grandma tottered off toward the kitchenette area of their little apartment, and I smiled. Hook, line, and sinker.

After she'd gone, Gus and I turned to each other. "Okay, talk. We probably don't have much time. How'd you know to come to the antique shop?"

Gus sighed. "Long story short, I own the shop. The alarm went off. I checked the security cameras on my phone app, saw what was happening, and figured I'd better get down there. I called Joey and told him to meet me."

My eyes widened. "Wait, you own the shop?" I hissed as loudly as one could hiss. I glanced toward the kitchen, then continued, "Elaborate."

He shrugged. "I own the damn antique shop. A lot of antiques are more than just old books or knick knacks, so I like to keep my finger on the pulse of the antique trade around here. Never know when something interesting will pop up, and boy, did it ever this time." He shook his head, chuckling. I, however, did not find this funny in the least.

"How did Mac and Regina end up with the trunk then? Was that planned?" I asked, whispering.

Grandma hummed in the kitchen as she made my sandwich. "Cricket! Do you want turkey or ham?" Grandma called out.

"Turkey!" I yelled back, then motioned for Gus to keep talking.

"No! It wasn't planned. That trunk from an estate sale showed up unexpectedly. By the time I found out it was from a descendant of the Caveden witches, my shop clerk had already sold it, and I didn't know who had bought it. I had been trying to track it down, casting different locator spells and all, but it's hard to do when you don't even know what the hell you're looking for." He shook his head as he spoke, obviously annoyed by the situation.

"Hell of a coincidence that Mac and her best friend, who just happens to be a descendant of the Cavedens, bought the trunk." I raised an eyebrow at him.

"Cricket, magical items have a way of finding their people," he said with a shrug as if that explained everything.

I rolled my eyes while Grandma came bouncing out of the kitchen with my sandwich. She placed it on the coffee table in front of me, beaming.

I smiled and picked it up, taking a tiny bite. "Mmmmm," I murmured as I chewed. Gus and I weren't done, not even close, so I had to get her out of here again. "So good, Grandma. Do you have any sweet tea? I could really go for some right now." Gus chuckled to himself, his shoulders quaking with silent laughter.

Grandma scowled. "Well, no... but I can make a batch! Do you have time to wait?"

"Of course, your sweet tea is worth the wait." I was laying it on thick, but it was working.

She grinned from ear to ear. "I guess I'd better get started then!" She smiled at Gus and headed back to the kitchen as he shook his head and watched her go.

"Anyway," I said, "what aren't you telling me about Revealers. Obviously, there's more to it than just being a supernatural radar detector. And is Mac one too?"

He sighed. "To tell you the truth, I don't know if she is or not. I know she has some latent powers. We'll just have to wait and see."

"Great," I huffed. "What about me? What are you not telling me?"

"I didn't *not* tell you on purpose, Cricket. I just figured, the less you knew, the better. You know, so you wouldn't worry about it."

"I'm not feeling reassured. Spill." My stomach dropped, feeling empty despite the few bites of the turkey sandwich I just consumed.

"Revealers are few and far between. Not a lot is known about them. So, it may not even happen to you," he said, fidgeting a bit with the zipper on his Members Only jacket.

"What, Gus? Just say it."

"Historically, the few Revealers that are in the record books had developed certain... powers..." he trailed off, and I raised my eyebrows at him, indicating he should get on with it.

"Such as?"

"Dark powers. Dark magic." He looked at me from behind those damned sunglasses he wore constantly.

"Dark magic. Are you saying I used dark magic when I took Stefan down with that mysterious light ball? Because that didn't feel 'dark' to me." My mind raced, trying to figure out what this actually meant.

"I'm not sure. There's not much to go on, but I think we need to keep a close eye on your powers as they develop.

"Stephan knows something. He kept referring to 'you Revealers' as if he has known quite a few. He said we're 'vile.'"

Gus shrugged. "It's possible. Dragons live hundreds of years. Maybe he has known a few in the past." I hadn't considered that Stephan was that old. I wondered how old Aiden actually was.

"So, all we can do is wait and see?" I asked, feeling quite annoyed.

"Yep. That's what I'm saying." He adjusted his glasses, then held his hands up and shrugged.

Grandma came back into the living room then, looking pleased with herself. "The tea is brewing. Won't be long now!" She sat down beside me and patted my knee.

"Actually, Grandma, I'm gonna have to go. Work stuff, I'm sorry," I said apologetically. I actually felt a little bad about making her go to the trouble of making sweet tea for me now.

"Oh no! Well, let me at least grab a Coke for you," she said, tottering off to the kitchen once again.

"By the way, Cricket, what in the hell triggered you to manifest a ball of energy to throw at Stephan? That kind of thing isn't easy to do." Gus cocked his head at me as if in awe of what I had done.

I shrugged, crossing my arms. "Remember when I supposedly 'passed out' at Essie's place that time? I had forgotten exactly what happened that night until Stephan was coming for Mac. The minute he put his hands on her, it came back to me." I paused and took a deep breath. "When I opened the door to that bedroom in Essie's apartment, I saw Stephan there in his dragon form. He had photos of Mac and Regina taped to the walls, along with other paperwork and photos. He had been planning this for some time, to take my daughter away from me. When I remembered that, and he touched her, I snapped."

Gus smiled, shaking his head. "Nothing like a mother's wrath for manifesting energy balls, eh?"

17

I sat in one of the pristine white chairs in front of Carl's desk in his office at Sunshine Cleaners. As usual, Alexandra had shown me in, and I was waiting for Carl to finish an email, or whatever he was doing, and acknowledge me. I had a lot to fill him in on, and I always felt nervous in his presence. As if I was always one wrong answer away from having his fangs buried in my neck. I took a deep breath as he put the lid of his laptop down, steepled his hands underneath his chin, and leveled those whiskey-colored eyes of his at me.

"Cricket, I heard about the showdown with the dragon shifter. Nicely done." A suggestion of a smile turned up one corner of his mouth as he looked at me with what seemed like a newfound respect.

"Yeah, thanks. About that. I really don't know how that happened."

Carl chuckled. "Relax. If you're worried that I think you've been keeping your powers secret from me, that's not the case. We knew you were a baby Revealer when we brought you on. It's only natural that your powers would continue to evolve over time. This is actually a welcomed development." He looked at me with one of those genial smiles you reserve for people you don't really like but have to tolerate.

I exhaled. "Okay, good. Because I didn't know. Anyway, as you know, Stephan is in critical condition in the ICU, and I've been told that he may have lost his ability to shift altogether after what I... did... to him." I stopped and cleared my throat while Carl grinned, clearly enjoying my discomfort. "And Aiden is gone now, too. So, the dragon situation has been dealt with, for now anyway." I quirked my brow at him, a slight grin playing on my lips.

Carl leaned back in his chair, toying with an ink pen and staring at me with something that looked an awful lot like awe. "Yes, well done, Cricket. Now we can get back to the main issue, which is finding out why supernatural beings from every corner of the earth are still congregating here, in Metro Nashville."

I nodded. "On it."

He continued to stare at me, then added, "We may need to reevaluate your position and salary. Considering your recently acquired skills, the MVA is more determined than ever to keep you in our employment. Whatever the cost might be."

I gulped. I didn't know how to respond to that.

He tossed the pen onto his desk and stood. "Ah, well. We can discuss that at a later time then. Have a good night, Cricket. You did well."

AFTER I LEFT Carl's office, I stopped in The Rusty Nail. Joey texted me earlier to let me know he was covering a shift tonight, and we hadn't talked since I told Zeb I needed some time. It would be good to see him before he had to head back to Kentucky to take care of pack business.

I walked in and spotted him behind the bar, a white towel draped over one shoulder, as usual when he was working. He smiled brightly at a patron while mixing a drink. When he spotted me, his smile transformed into something more intimate, meant only for me. I melted right then and there.

I made my way toward the bar and took a seat at the far end, watching Joey work. He glanced my way once in a while, winking or giving me a knowing smile, which set the butterflies in my stomach into flight. Finally, he moved to my end of the bar and sat a shot of vodka in front of me.

"That's on the house," he said with a smile.

"Bottoms up then," I said, downing the shot while he chuckled.

"Nice cast, Dragon Slayer," he said with a chuckle, nodding at the cast on my arm with Mac's purple writing on it.

I rolled my eyes. "Yeah, I have Mac to thank for that."

"I'm glad you stopped in. I was supposed to head back to New Haven this morning, but since they needed help covering a couple of shifts, I said I'd stay a few more days."

I grinned. "I'm certainly not complaining about you staying in town."

"Good. Because I'll be back to stay before you know it." He winked and wiped the bar in front of me with the towel before replacing it on his shoulder.

Something inside of me started buzzing when I heard that, making me feel warm and flushed. *Stop it*, Logical Cricket demanded. *You just told Zeb you needed some time, so take some time.* Ho Cricket peeked out of the closet just then. *I don't know. Some time spent with Joey sounds nice.*

I decided I'd better just tell him and get it over with. "So, remember last time we talked? About Zeb?" My finger traced the rim of the empty shot glass that still sat in front of me.

"Yeah..."

"I told him I needed some time. By myself. To think about things," I stammered, feeling nervous suddenly. I bit the inside of my lip.

"Oh," he said, shoving his hands into the pockets of his jeans. "Well, that's probably a good idea. You seemed like you needed some time. You know, last time we talked." I tried not to smile as he spoke and continued watching my finger as it traced the rim of the shot glass instead.

"Yeah."

"Well, maybe we can hang out sometime when I'm back in town. I mean, if you want to." His head tilted down, but he met my gaze through his lashes. He was being cute and kind of bashful, and I was surprised at how much I liked this side of him.

"I'd like that. Very much." I grinned and watched as a smile tugged the corners of Joey's mouth upward.

He nodded. "Okay, then."

"Bloody hell! I should've known," a familiar voice cut through the normal sounds of the bar and the music blaring from the jukebox. Zeb.

Oh, shit.

18

Zeb entered the bar, his loud voice booming. Everyone turned to stare as he made his way toward the end of the bar where Joey and I were. He staggered a bit, his eyes red and bloodshot, his flannel shirt looking wrinkled and disheveled. I stared in disbelief as he approached us, his eyes dark and blazing.

"So, this is why you 'needed time'? To fuck Joey?" he asked, his words slurred and using air quotes as he spoke.

"Hey, man, settle down." Joey tossed his towel onto the bar and walked around to stand on my side of it, getting between Zeb and me.

"I trusted you, believed it when you said you two were only friends. You've probably been fucking all along. You made a bloody cuck out of me, Cricket."

"Zeb! No, that's not—" I began, but Joey cut me off.

"Get the fuck out of here. I'll call you a cab. You're drunk. Go home before you say something you'll really regret." Joey took his phone out of his back pocket and started scrolling to find a number for a taxi, I assumed.

"I don't need you to call me a cab. I don't need anything

from either of you." Zeb stared at me as he said it, and my heart shattered.

"Yeah, well, I don't need you making a scene in my bar or talking to Cricket like that. Get the hell out of here."

I looked around to see that, indeed, nearly everyone in the bar was watching the three of us.

Clearly, Zeb was drunk and in his feelings. He'd taken this much worse than I thought he would, and a wave of guilt washed over me. He was in pain and acting out of that hurt right now. "Zeb, let me take you home, okay?" I asked gently, placing a hand on his arm.

He shrugged me off. "I said I don't need anything from you, and I meant it. You should go home, Cricket. Joseph and I need to have a talk." He looked at Joey while he spoke, anger sparking in his eyes as he swayed where he stood. I felt the familiar crackling heat of his Reaper aura in the air and knew he meant to do more than just talk to Joey.

"We'll talk when you're sober, man. Right now, you need to go sleep it off."

Zeb took a step closer to Joey, getting in his face, his eyes dark. He put the palm of his hand on Joey's shoulder, giving him a little shove backward.

"Dude..." Joey said, dragging the word out as if giving Zeb one last warning. My heart raced. I sensed static electricity in the air, the signature of Joey's wolf side.

"Zeb, please." I tugged on his arm, trying to make him look at me, but he refused. He trained his murderous glare on Joey as he again shook me off roughly.

Again, he pushed Joey. Joey pushed him back, causing Zeb to stumble back a bit. Zeb grabbed a nearby chair and righted himself, his expression becoming darker than I'd ever seen before. I didn't have time to say or do anything else to diffuse the situation. Zeb crashed into Joey, his fist connecting with Joey's face. Some patrons screamed, a few of them rushing the door to get out of the bar. I noticed a couple of guys near the pool tables wearing black T-shirts with "SECURITY" on the front. They put their cue sticks down and headed toward us.

Joey fought back, giving as good as he got. He punched Zeb in the face, then the stomach. Zeb grabbed a beer bottle from a nearby table, smashing it over Joey's head. Joey groaned, then slammed Zeb into the jukebox, which brought the music to a screeching halt in protest of the abuse. Zeb kicked one foot out, landing it right into Joey's stomach. I stood back, one hand to my mouth, watching them in disbelief.

The security guys began to intervene, one on each of them. One of them tried holding Zeb back by his biceps, but he shrugged out of the guy's grip effortlessly, then went after Joey again. The other one had Joey around the waist, trying to pull him away, but Joey lunged at Zeb, carrying the security guy along with him.

"Stop! Stop it!" I yelled, but I didn't think they even heard me over the commotion. Patrons were still screaming and yelling, either trying to escape the bar or gathering close around the action and cheering them on. A few even had their phones out, holding them up to get a better angle of the brawl.

By this time, they'd fought their way over by the pool tables, and Zeb grabbed a cue stick, breaking it over Joey's head. Joey tackled Zeb onto the green felt-covered table, where they grappled, landing punches to each other's faces. The guards were still trying in vain to pry them apart, not knowing they were dealing with a Reaper and a wolf shifter. The two of them grunted and groaned, rolling off the table and onto the floor, each of them dripping blood from various gashes they'd inflicted on one another.

I took advantage of the lull in the action to yell at them again, "Stop! STOP!" This time they heard me, each of them turning to me with their bruised, bloodied faces.

"Listen to the lady," one of the security guys said breathlessly as Zeb and Joey began to slow down.

Joey ran a hand through his tousled curls, breathing hard with blood trickling from his forehead and his lips. He slumped against the pool table, holding his side and wincing. Zeb collapsed into a nearby chair and put his head in his hands. Blood dripped to the floor from his face as he sat there, catching his breath.

"Damn it, Zeb." Joey glared at him, then at the destruction surrounding us. The jukebox was smashed, the felt covering on the pool table was ripped and soiled with blood, chairs and tables lay turned over and broken all over the bar. A few patrons remained, a couple with their cell phones out, grinning as they scrolled and tapped on them. I made a mental note to check YouTube later to see if Zeb and Joey had gone viral.

I threw my hands up in the air. "I can't believe the two of you!" I stormed out of the bar, leaving them both to lick their own wounds.

THE NEXT MORNING I awoke to a soft knock on my door. I opened my eyes to find I had been asleep in the recliner in the living room, still wearing my shoes even. I rubbed my eyes as the knock sounded again and got up to see who was at my door this early on a Sunday morning.

"Hi... Good morning." Zeb stood there, looking sheepishly at me. His face was swollen with green and yellow rings under both eyes. His lip was split and scabbed over; he winced when he spoke. It had only been a few hours since the fight, but I suspected his face would be healed completely within the next twenty-four hours. He looked like he hadn't slept at all as he stood there with a Krispy Kreme bag and a cup of coffee. He held them out to me.

The night's events came rushing back to me, and I was instantly annoyed again. "Zeb—" I shook my head.

"Wait, please. I came here to say I'm sorry. I was a right arsehole last night—and the last few weeks, if we're honest. I didn't mean what I said last night, either. You need time. I understand that now. Take all the time you need. I'm not going anywhere, and I'm not giving up," he said, struggling to form the words with his split lip. He held the bag and the coffee out to me again, and I accepted them.

I bit the inside of my lip and studied him for a moment. "I forgive you. But Zeb, I've tried to be honest with you—and Joey—all along, about my feelings and—"

"It's okay, Cricket. You don't have to explain. I fucked up last night. You don't owe me any explanations. When I saw you there, with Joey, and you were smiling at him like that... It caught me off guard." He stopped and let out a heavy sigh, running his hands through his blond, spiky hair. "I just wanted to say I'm sorry, and I'll still be here whenever you're ready." He smiled softly, as much as he could with the swollen lip, and backed away. I watched him disappear into his side of the duplex, then I retreated into my side with the breakfast he'd brought me.

I took a sip of the coffee—divine—and pulled out a doughnut. Chocolate creme-filled—my favorite. I took a bite and moaned. It was so good. I thought about Zeb's apology, considering what had happened last night, and my spirits lifted. It seemed he was willing to give me the time I needed to figure things out, and he realized he had been wrong. The guilt I'd been carrying about breaking up with him lifted, and I felt free.

Free to be myself. To figure out what I wanted, who I wanted.

As I WAS GETTING ready for bed that night, feeling relatively content, my phone rang. I stopped applying moisturizer to my face and grabbed it. "I'm a Werewolf, Baby" by The Tragically Hip tipped me off that it was Joey. I bit my lip and grinned as I answered it.

"Hey, Joe. What's up?"

"Babe, you're still up! Would you mind if I stopped by for a few?"

I looked at myself in the mirror, sans makeup, hair in a messy bun, wearing my pajama short set and robe. I sighed. He's probably seen me looking worse, to be honest. "Sure, come on by."

He said he'd be at my place in less than ten minutes, so after we hung up, I rushed around tidying up the living room and making myself look as presentable as possible. Mac was upstairs, already asleep in her room. I peeked out my window and saw that Zeb's bike was gone. He was either out working or—I didn't want to finish that thought. But at least he wouldn't be around for this. I didn't want to rub salt in his wounds.

Soon, I heard a soft knock at the door. I opened it to find Joey standing there looking as hot as usual. His brown curls a bit tousled, his russet brown eyes smoldering. He wore jeans, a black, form-fitting T-shirt, and a leather jacket. He looked no worse for wear after the bar fight with Zeb last night. His werewolf healing abilities had apparently taken care of all his injuries. His lips turned up in a sexy smile as he looked me over. I suddenly felt self-conscious about not changing out of my pajamas as the butterflies in my stomach took flight.

"Hi, babe." His voice was low and rumbly, making his southern drawl even more pronounced.

"Hi." I opened the door wider to allow him in, and he brushed against me as he came inside, sending a warm sensation through every part of me.

He turned to face me, hands shoved into his pockets. "Cricket, I wanted to apologize in person. I shouldn't have let Zeb get to me, I know you'd just broken up with him, and he was hurt... and I let him push my buttons. I'm sorry." He quirked his lips to one side and raised an eyebrow. "Can you forgive me?"

I smiled, nodding. "Yes, I forgive you. I forgave Zeb too. He stopped by earlier. It's all good."

He sighed, a relieved smile washing over his face. "Good. I'm glad he apologized to you, too. Although, he could apologize to me also," he said, grinning, and I laughed.

"I'm sure he will, eventually." I wished once again that I'd changed back into regular clothes before Joey got here, but there was nothing to do about it now. "Want to sit down? Can I get you a beer?"

"No, thanks. I won't stay long. You're probably ready for bed." I saw his eyes darken as he said that last part, and that sent a shock of electricity straight to my core. "I just noticed Zeb was downtown. There was an attempted suicide, and I guess he got called in for that. So, I figured I'd stop by while the coast was clear," he said with a sly grin.

"Okay. Well, I'm glad you stopped by." I bit the inside of

my lip as we stood there awkwardly for a couple of beats.

"Would you want to—"

"When are you—"

We both started talking at the same time, which made us both laugh.

"You first," I said.

He licked his lips nervously, which I found adorable. "Okay. Well, I was just going to ask if you might want to hang out when I get back? I'm leaving tomorrow for New Haven. They've finally found a replacement Alpha, and we're going to make it official next week. Then I'll be free to come back to Nashville," he said, his eyes sparkling as he spoke. "If you want, we could—you know, hang out."

I pursed my lips, trying to conceal my smile. I nodded, then met his eyes. "Mr. Morley, are you asking me on a date?"

"Oh, I don't know. Maybe? I mean, would that be okay?" he said, floundering, and I burst out laughing.

"Yes. That would be more than okay. I'd love to."

He cocked his head, smiling. "Really? I mean, I'd understand if you just want to be by yourself for a while."

"I'm taking some time for myself. That includes figuring out what I want—who I want. And what I want right now is to spend some more time with you. I want to get to know you better, Joey. We've been friends a long time, but I still feel like I don't really know you."

A slow smile spread across his face, and he nodded, glancing down shyly. "Okay, then. I want that too."

"Good, it's settled then." I bit my lip as he looked up at me.

"I guess I'll call you when I'm back."

"You'd better."

We stood there staring and smiling for a couple of

seconds, like two teenagers with a crush on each other.

"I should go." Joey made a move toward the door, then he stopped and turned toward me.

Within seconds, his mouth was on mine, one hand entangled in my hair at the base of my neck, the other sliding down my side to rest at my hip. I kissed him back, meeting his intensity with my own, gliding my arms up around his neck. His tongue parted my lips, finding mine, while my hands roamed up into his hair. Sparks flew inside of me, ricocheting throughout my body and settling in my core.

This felt good. Too good.

I broke the kiss, leaning into him and pressing my forehead against his. His thumbs stroked my hips where his hands had settled, holding me close to him, both of us trying to catch our breath.

"Plenty of time for that when I get back," he said breathlessly.

I nodded in agreement. "Definitely."

"So, I'll call you?" he asked, still close enough that we shared the same air.

"Call me."

He pressed one more kiss to my lips, then backed away. With a devilish smile, he was gone, leaving me a smoldering mess. I pressed my fingers to my lips, still tingling from his kiss. I was excited and eager to explore my feelings for Joey, finally. I owed it to myself, and to him, to find out if there was anything there before I committed to Zeb or anyone else for that matter.

I made sure the door was locked, turned off the lights, and headed upstairs to bed. I felt lighter than I had ever felt before, free to do what I wanted, finally. And I couldn't wait to start.

19

One week later, I stood in front of Grandma and Gus's door at Forever Young. Gus called me twenty minutes ago and asked me to rush over, so I did, not knowing what was wrong. I banged on the door again, fear rushing through my veins. What if something was wrong with Grandma?

Gus flung the door open, peering behind me, then down each side of the corridor before pulling me inside.

"What's going on, Gus?" I asked, looking around the apartment for Grandma. "Is something wrong with Grandma?"

"No, no. She's not here. She's at hot yoga." He turned the television off, then fidgeted with the remote, tossing it from one hand to the other. He looked out of sorts, not the usual grouchy but in charge Gus I knew so well.

"So, what's going on then? What was so urgent you needed me over here ASAP?" I asked, slightly annoyed there was no emergency.

"Alright, I guess I should just spit it out," he said, laying the remote down and turning to face me with those ever-present sunglasses covering his eyes. "They're coming for me, Cricket. I need help."

I blinked in surprise. "Coming for you? Who?"

He swept his arm out in an all-encompassing gesture. "All of them. They're coming to Nashville because I'm here. It happened in Prague, it happened in Sydney, it happened in Paris—that's why I left. They follow me everywhere I go." He collapsed onto the sofa and took off his fedora hat, slinging it onto the coffee table.

I thought for a moment before speaking, trying to make sense of what he said. "You mean all the supernatural beings that have been coming to Nashville? It's because of you?"

"Yes, that's what I'm saying!" he practically yelled.

"Okay, okay, settle down," I said, rolling my eyes. "But why would they follow you?"

He sighed. "There's a lot I haven't told you."

"You think?"

"I'm sorry. I didn't think it would happen again. I took preventative measures, but I guess they didn't work." He frowned.

"What do you think I can do about it?" I crossed my arms and cocked my head at him.

"Your powers, the way they're evolving. I think you're the answer I've been waiting for. We just have to work together to figure it out."

"So, you're telling me you've known my ultimate mission for the MVA all along and that it involved you. And you didn't say anything before now?"

"Can you focus here? We'll circle back to that," he said, waving me off.

I sighed heavily and stepped toward the door.

"Wait! Fine, sit down, and I'll tell you the abridged version."

I narrowed my eyes at him, then slowly made my way to the couch, sat down, and motioned with my hand for him to get on with it.

He took a deep breath, then began. "Back when I was younger—much younger—I went on an archaeology dig with my Uncle Phil in Greece, at the Mycenaean sites. We were digging near the ancient Palace of Nestor, near Pylos, and stumbled upon some burial sites. We spent the next six months uncovering all sorts of artifacts like gold cups, beads made from precious gemstones, ancient gold and silver jewelry—everything untouched, just like it was when they buried it."

Now, he had my attention. I cocked my head, listening intently.

"I found a silver pot while I was digging. I spent days uncovering it carefully so as not to damage it. I finally excavated it, and I was so excited, I didn't wait for anyone else. I wanted to know if anything was inside of it, so I pried the lid off—carefully—and saw a glowing amber liquid in it. Just a small amount and it behaved kind of like mercury. It was shiny, thin, and slippery."

He paused and shrugged, looking defeated. "I was young and stupid. I stuck my hand into the pot. The liquid rose up to meet my fingers like it had a mind of its own. Before I could pull my hand out of there, it latched onto my skin, absorbing into me. Within only a few seconds, it was done."

I stared, open-mouthed. "What? Do you mean it's still inside of you? Even now?"

Without answering me, Gus reached for his sunglasses.

The glasses he always wore, night or day, rain or shine. I'd never seen him without them. He pulled them off, and I recoiled at the amber glow that emanated from his irises.

"Oh, my God! Gus!" I gasped. I thought about Cyclops from the X-Men movies and how he emitted laser beams from his eyes and had to wear a special set of glasses to contain it. I figured I'd better not bring that up right now, though.

He put the glasses back on. "All I know is that whatever it is, it's some kind of ancient magic. It made me the powerful warlock I am, but it also makes me a target. They all want it, and that's why they're drawn here—to me. Even if they don't know it, they're drawn to it."

"So, how could they get it? It's inside of you. Oh." I answered my own question. Gus's life was in danger, he had been in danger for a long time.

He nodded at my realization. "I've been reading up on Revealers and your growing powers. I have a plan to get this thing out of me, but I need your help. And we're going to have to see if we can speed up this evolution of yours, too."

I balked. "Gus, I don't know. I mean, I don't—"

"Cricket. Please? You may be my only hope here."

I looked at the little, wrinkled man sitting on the couch across from me, looking helpless and confused. A far cry from the confident, cranky, powerful warlock I'd come to know.

"Okay, we can try, I guess. But why now? What's the urgency?"

He put one hand on his chest. "I can feel it, inside of me. And it's growing stronger all the time, especially over the last few weeks. I think it knows that someone very powerful is coming for me—for it, and soon."

I shook my head, taking my phone out of my bag. "Alright, well, let's let Carl know about this. He'll know—"

"NO! You can't tell him!" Gus interrupted me yet again.

"Why not?"

"I don't know what the MVA would do to me if they knew. We have to get it out of me first, then let them deal with... whatever it is."

I pursed my lips together, thinking. "I don't like this, Gus. How about this? We'll try to get it out of you on our own first. If it doesn't work, we tell Carl immediately."

"Alright, deal." He stood, smiling at me and pulling me up for a hug. "Thank you, Cricket. You don't know what this means to me. I'll be so glad to get rid of this thing."

"Don't thank me yet. I haven't done anything. Also, does Grandma know about your eyes?"

He scoffed, waving dismissively. "Nah, she thinks I have an eye condition that requires me to wear dark glasses all the time. God love her. That woman is a saint, I'll tell you."

"That she is," I agreed as I headed toward the door.

"Go home, get some rest, come back tomorrow morning. We'll get started first thing."

"Okay, but you'd better have coffee and doughnuts," I warned as he shut the door behind me.

Something told me I was going to regret agreeing to this.

Nashville Immortals Book Four – Beckoning Shadows – coming soon!

Sign up for news and updates about Beckoning Shadows!

https://shaunajaredauthor.myflodesk.com/
beckoningshadowsupdates

AND PLEASE JOIN my newsletter to stay up to date on future books and other news... and also for free books and give-aways! Sign up here!

https://shaunajaredauthor.myflodesk.com/sjnewsletter

PLEASE LEAVE A REVIEW AND FOLLOW ME!

I hope you've enjoyed Burning Secrets! Thanks so much for reading! Please consider leaving a review on Amazon, Goodreads, BookBub, etc. Reviews help indie authors by giving their books more visibility because the more reviews a book has, the more Amazon shows it to potential readers! Blogging and posting about books on your social media accounts are also great and very appreciated ways to spread the word about books you loved!

I love to hear from my readers, and I mostly hang out on Instagram and Facebook, so please feel free to follow me, DM me, and join my reader group on Facebook!

instagram.com/shaunajaredauthor
    instagram.com/authorshaunajared
    facebook.com/shaunajaredauthor

Facebook Reader Group: https://www.facebook.com/groups/1020073908355059

And please join my newsletter to stay up to date on future books and other news... and also for free books and give-aways! Sign up here!

https://shaunajaredauthor.myflodesk.com/sjnewsletter

ALSO BY THE AUTHOR

Nashville Immortals Series – Paranormal Women's Fiction Romance

Bitter End – https://books2read.com/SJBE

Bad Blood – https://books2read.com/SJBB

Burning Secrets – https://books2read.com/SJBS

Beckoning Shadows - coming soon – sign up to be the first to know! https://shaunajaredauthor.myflodesk.com/beckoningshadowsupdates

Tennessee Whiskey Series – Steamy Contemporary Romance

Southern Poison – https://books2read.com/SJSP

Southern Heat – https://books2read.com/SJSH

Southern Honey – coming soon – sign up to be the first to know!

https://shaunajaredauthor.myflodesk.com/southernhoneyupdates

Visit my website at www.shaunajaredauthor.com to find out more about my Kindle Vella serial stories and more!

ABOUT THE AUTHOR

Shauna is a romance author who aspires to become a professional time traveler. She has written a contemporary romance with two installments so far, the Tennessee Whiskey series, including Southern Poison and Southern Heat. She also has a paranormal women's fiction romance series, Nashville Immortals, with three books published currently. Shauna is hard at work on her next books, book three in the Tennessee Whiskey trilogy and the fourth installment in Nashville Immortals. She writes about all things romance and lives vicariously through her characters.

Shauna lives near Nashville, TN with her husband, son, and their dog. She loves books, coffee, wine, and bacon, in no particular order.

www.shaunajaredauthor.com